MW01634322

SHIELDING AALIYAH (SPECIAL FORCES: OPERATION ALPHA)

DELTA FORCE - GENERATION NEXT, BOOK 2

JEN TALTY

Dear Readers,

Welcome to the Special Forces: Operation Alpha Fan-Fiction world!

If you are new to this amazing world, in a nutshell the author wrote a story using one or more of my characters in it. Sometimes that character has a major role in the story, and other times they are only mentioned briefly. This is perfectly legal and allowable because they are going through Aces Press to publish the story.

This book is entirely the work of the author who wrote it. While I might have assisted with brainstorming and other ideas about which of my characters to use, I didn't have any part in the process or writing or editing the story.

I'm proud and excited that so many authors loved my characters enough that they wanted to write them into their own story. Thank you for supporting them, and me!

READ ON!

Xoxo

Susan Stoker

hearts as the memorable characters take you on a healing journey of love. A mysterious death brings danger and intrigue into the drama, while sultry passions brew into a believable plot that melts the reader's heart. Jen Talty pens an entertaining romance that grips the heart as the colorful and dangerous story unfolds into a chilling ending." *Night Owl Reviews*

"This is not the typical love story, nor is it the typical mystery. The characters are well rounded and interesting." *You Gotta Read Reviews*

"*Murder in Paradise Bay* is a fast-paced romantic thriller with plenty of twists and turns to keep you guessing until the end. You won't want to miss this one..." *USA Today bestselling author Janice Maynard*

Welcome to *The Next Generation* of Delta Force. This series will focus on the men and women related to Susan Stoker's characters in her *Delta Team* and *Delta Team Two* series. In this first book is Aaliyah Rose who is cousins with Jayme Caldwell from *Shielding Jayme (Delta Team Two Book 4)* and her husband Rocket Long. Also making an appearance is Porter "Oz" Reed from *Shielding Riley (Delta Team Two book 5)*.

Check out my other series inside Susan Stoker's world: *The Airforce Fire Protection* series and *the Search and Rescue* series.

Now grab a glass of vino (or whatever your favorite drink is) and kick back, relax, and let the romance roll in!

CHAPTER 1

Aaliyah Rose zigzagged through the airport, dodging people left and right, trying not to hit them with her backpack. Her heart pounded in her chest as if she were at the tail end of the Boston Marathon, sprinting toward the finish line. Something she'd never do. Not in a million fucking years. It wasn't that she was against exercise. Nope. She did that daily. Yoga. Kickboxing. Tennis. Even pickleball. Just not running. Power walking? Or hiking? Sure. She loved being on the beach or climbing a mountain. Or even a roadside as long as there was something nice to look at.

But running was something she could never understand.

She blew out a long breath.

Her mind filled with anything and everything from her childhood in Texas so that she didn't have to think about Huck.

Huckleberry Duncan.

She couldn't believe he'd landed in Killeen, Texas, of all places.

Not that Huck had any control where Delta Force sent him, and according to Jayme, he wasn't on the same team as her husband, Rocket, but their paths had crossed since the two teams did training exercises together on a regular basis. Jayme, however, had yet to meet him and that was okay because the last thing Aaliyah needed was for Huck to be warned that Aaliyah was on her way into town.

Quickly, she glanced at her cell. Jayme had texted that they were pulling up and should be there any second.

Butterflies filled her stomach. She hadn't been this nervous since she signed up for the spelling bee in the sixth grade just so she could spend time with Tommy Sabre, the cutest and smartest boy in the entire class.

It had come down to Aaliyah and Tommy in the last round and she had to let him win. And she did.

Only it didn't do her any good. Candy, the prettiest girl in school, ended up going to the dance with Tommy. Not because she did well in the contest—she hadn't even entered—but because she sat in the front row, looking all adorable, and cheered him on like a groupie.

So much for trying to impress someone with her mind.

She continued toward the passenger pickup signs. With every step her pulse increased.

In a few short hours, Aaliyah would be face-to-face with the only man she'd ever really loved.

Last Aaliyah had heard, Huck had been stationed in South Carolina before being transferred to Texas. Of course, he wouldn't take her calls. Actually, he'd changed his number. And all her letters had been returned.

Unopened.

He had written in big block letters on a piece of paper. *Don't contact me ever again.*

That said it all. But Aaliyah couldn't let his silence continue. Nor could she let him continue to blame her, and himself, for his brother's death. There was so much that needed to be explained and all she asked for was that he listened. He need not say a single word when she was done if he didn't want to. If he still felt the need to walk away, then so be it. She had no control over what he did with the information she presented him with.

She might have stabbed Sawyer with the knife that ended his life, but if she hadn't, Huck's life would be over. He might not be dead, but his career would have been ruined and if Sawyer had been able to execute his plan, Huck would have been in jail.

And she would be dead.

Huck hadn't been able to see past what he thought happened instead of looking at the bigger picture. She needed to show him that.

Aaliyah made her way into the baggage claim area, but she had no luggage to collect. Jayme had called yesterday, informing her that now would be a good time to come since there was a lull in the team's action. Aaliyah didn't care about the cost. She found herself on the next flight. She'd buy whatever she needed when she got herself settled. That was if she stayed more than a day or two.

She adjusted her backpack over her shoulder and stepped outside. She squinted, looking for Rocket's SUV. Jayme and Rocket had been married for twelve years and they had two adorable little children.

Not that Aaliyah had ever met them, but Jayme was good at sending pictures on a regular basis. Connor was going on ten and Kayleigh was about to turn nine. It wasn't that Jayme and Aaliyah weren't close, but until a year ago, Aaliyah spent most of her time hiding behind big sunglasses, large hats, and inches of thick makeup. And she never dared to return to her hometown. Never. Hell, she didn't travel, not unless Sawyer had made her and that wasn't very often. The shame of being beaten on a regular basis had taken its toll on all her other relationships.

Until she met Sawyer's brother.

Huck had changed everything.

He made her want to be a different person; only, she hadn't been honest about who she was and when the shit hit the fan, it was all too late to explain everything.

"Aaliyah!" Jayme stuck her head out the window and waved frantically.

Tapping her foot against the pavement, Aaliyah waited as patiently as she could for Rocket to pull his vehicle to the side. She pulled open the rear passenger door, expecting to be greeted by her grandniece and nephew. She frowned. "Where's Connor and Kayleigh?"

"Well, aren't you excited to see me?" Jayme asked with a pouty face.

"Of course I am." Aaliyah leaned forward and hugged her cousin. There was a good fifteen-year difference in age and growing up, Aaliyah barely ever saw Jayme, but ever since Sawyer's death, they'd become close.

And Aaliyah certainly needed a friend.

"I was just excited to see your adorable kiddos in person instead of photographs."

Jayme laughed. "They are only adorable these days when they're sleeping or when on the rare occasion they are behaving like little angels instead of little devils with attitudes the size of this great state."

"Sounds like they take after Memaw."

"You have no idea," Rocket said.

"You remember my husband." Jayme reached across the front of the SUV and patted Rocket's shoulder.

"I haven't seen you since right after the wedding." Aaliyah had been twenty when Jayme had tied the knot. Six months later, she spent a semester abroad and ended up finding a sales job with a company that had offices all over the globe. She took a position in Singapore where she met Sawyer, who happened to be her boss.

That should have been her first red flag.

Never date your boss.

And not just because he's in a position of power, though in this case, that should have been reason enough.

The last time Aaliyah had been to Texas had been right before her memaw had passed. Jayme and Rocket had been out of town on vacation. Aaliyah had picked that time frame on purpose. She didn't want many family members asking too many questions about why she didn't come around too often or call much anymore.

She'd been lucky that Sawyer agreed to let her visit at all and that had been under protest. She had to beg and she'd used her ninety-something memaw to do it.

May she rest in peace.

Had Winnie Morrison known that Sawyer Duncan had even laid a hand on her once, she would have taken care of the situation and it wouldn't have been called self-defense.

Aaliyah had no regrets for that visit. She could still feel the sting of her husband's backhand coming across the side of her face, followed by a quick jab to her ribs. When she asked why he hit her that time, she hadn't done anything wrong, he smiled and said, *"Because you left. That's reason enough. Don't do it again."*

"A lot has changed." Rocket glanced over his shoulder. "I'm sorry for everything you've gone though."

"Thanks. I appreciate it." A tightness filled her chest. After Sawyer died, Jayme flew to Manhattan and spent three weeks holding Aaliyah's hand while she told the police what happened. And then repeated the story when they returned for clarification. Jayme held her while she cried into the night and raced to her bedside when the nightmares jarred her awake.

"I'm even more sorry that we didn't see the signs," he said as the SUV eased back into traffic.

"I hid them quite well." She didn't want to have this conversation again, but she understood that for those that loved her the most, they needed to have it and sometimes more than once. And every time they brought it up, she would forever remind them that she did everything she could to bury her dirty little secret. She learned to pretend that her life was as rich as her husband's bank account. On the outside, it appeared she lived the kind of lifestyle others could only dream about. Fancy cars. Private jets. Glam squad, when her husband deemed it necessary.

But it was all for show.

On the inside, her world was a war zone.

The only way to survive had been to push people away, and that's what she'd done with Jayme and everyone else in her life for that matter.

"I became a master at covering up both my emotional scars and my physical scars."

Jayme reached from the front seat to the back. She took Aaliyah's hand and squeezed. "You mastered keeping all of us at a distance. You became the queen of pissing people off. You were so good at it that we all thought you disliked us. I'm ashamed to admit this, but I even told Memaw that you were a hopeless, selfish bitch who only cared about your money."

"That's what I wanted you to believe." Tears welled in Aaliyah's eyes. When she was living in the middle of all the insanity, it felt as though she had no choice. She believed the control Sawyer had was all-consuming. All powerful. No one could help.

But that's what Sawyer had done to her ability to think for herself. He stole every inch of her worth. She sucked in a deep breath. Even in death he had reach.

No. She would no longer give him that kind of control. She was in charge of her own destiny now.

Her life belonged only to her now.

"I wish I understood that you were hiding pain and shame. I failed you."

"No. You didn't." Aaliyah leaned closer and kissed her cousin's cheek. "Even if you knew and confronted me about what was going on, I would have lied. I would have made excuses. I still would have stayed with him because I didn't know how to leave."

"Until Huck showed up," Jayme said.

Aaliyah sat back and pulled the seat belt tight across her lap. She adjusted her sunglasses and stared out the window at the Texas landscape. When Aaliyah had left her hometown, she'd been a bright-eyed and bushy-tailed young woman who was going to go out in the world and make her mark.

She had goals.

Which included becoming a millionaire.

So for her family to call her a self-absorbed bitch who didn't care about anyone else but herself—well, it fit. At least on the outside looking in because when she'd been a young girl starting out, she had dollar signs in her eyes and she wasn't concerned about coming home for Christmas. Hell, she wasn't concerned about the holidays unless it meant a fatter paycheck and possibly a promotion.

She didn't even care that people in the office hated her and accused her of sleeping her way to the top.

Because it wasn't entirely false.

Everything she did was calculated.

Her assistant once called her conniving and manipulative and Aaliyah took that as a compliment. She didn't get to be one of the top salespeople in her first three years by playing nice in the sandbox. Even when she'd first met Sawyer, she'd used him and he got off on that idea. He was mildly amused by her ambition.

Until the topic of marriage came about.

And then children.

No wife of his was going to work. That's how he put it at first. As things progressed, he made it more clear with his fists.

"Even then I made a mess of things." Aaliyah sucked in a deep breath. She held it for a count of ten before letting it out slowly. If she could go back and change that very first meeting, she would. Not so much because she regretted falling in love with Huck. She didn't. But sleeping with him and not telling him she was his brother's wife had been the biggest mistake of her life. Had she been honest, maybe Huck wouldn't hate her today. "All I want is a chance to explain. He never gave me that." She turned her attention toward Rocket. "Does he talk about his brother? About me?"

"We're not on the same team, though we do a lot of training together," Rocket said. "But that's pretty intense so we don't usually socialize at the base much. But we do occasionally get together for a beer." Rocket glanced in the rearview mirror. "However, he's never mentioned his brother. Or how he died."

"Has anyone asked him about his family or anything?" Aaliyah asked.

"Sure, but he says his parents are dead and leaves it at that, so no one pushes," Rocket said.

"Isn't he close to Tony's brother?" Jayme asked.

"As close as Huck is to anyone." Rocket nodded. "You'll meet Cannon and his fiancée, Jolene, at our house tonight."

"I can't believe you're having an impromptu gathering so I can corner Huck." Part of Aaliyah felt guilty as fuck for her approach. However, she felt strongly that Huck owed her the time it took for her to explain how things happened, especially what he hadn't been present for and what his brother had done.

More importantly, what his brother had planned and the proof she held.

If Huck knew that, maybe he could find it in his heart to forgive. That's all she wanted. She knew he'd never take her back and she'd accepted that. Even if he couldn't forgive, at least she'd been heard.

That would be enough.

She could go back to her life knowing she'd given Huck the truth. He deserved to know. At least that's what she kept telling herself because in part, she needed this for herself too.

Rocket turned off the highway and rolled to a stop at a light. Like everything in Texas, the land was flat and on a grid. "I invited everyone from both teams, which we have done before since Cannon is Tony's little brother."

"But wait. Isn't Tony a schoolteacher?" If memory served her correctly, he'd been Connor's teacher.

Rocket chuckled. "He is, but he was once one of us, which means he's always one of us."

"I've heard that." The closer they got to Jayme's neighborhood, the faster Aaliyah's heart beat.

This was it. This was what she'd been dreaming about doing for months. She'd practiced her speech over and over again, both in her mind and in front of her mirror. She knew it inside and out. Every detail she wanted to cover. Every ugly truth she needed to reveal.

Even the ones about herself.

But especially the ones about Sawyer.

She clutched her backpack. She had the proof, but would Huck listen and believe? Or would he think this was some last-ditch effort to win him back or make her look less like a killer?

Dropping her head back, she squeezed her eyes shut. She still loved Huck and if she was being completely honest with herself, she'd always love him. That was a fact she'd never be able to change. He was her soulmate. She knew that the second they locked eyes in that bar.

But she also knew he was done with her and that happened two weeks later when he waltzed into her home and found out she was his brother's wife. The look on his face was as if someone took a cattle prod and shoved it down his throat. Once the shock wore off, he plastered a fake smile on his face and pretended to be interested in her life with Sawyer, all while anger filled his glare.

Of course, she'd been just as surprised. She'd thought he'd left town. That his leave had been all used up before Sawyer had made it back from Singapore.

However, there had been so much she hadn't known.

Like how Sawyer knew about her affair and what he planned on doing. That juicy piece of information came in the form of a fist sandwich seconds after Huck left that evening.

"We're here," Jayme said.

Aaliyah sat up taller. She pushed her glasses on top of her head and wiped the few tears from her cheeks that had escaped her eyes. "Wow. Your home is beautiful."

"Thanks." Jayme smiled. It was bright and beaming and she looked like she was the happiest woman in the world.

Aaliyah wasn't jealous. She wasn't even envious.

She just wished that someday she'd have even a teeny-tiny piece of the life that her cousin had, though she knew it would never happen and she had no one to blame but herself.

"The kids are at a neighbor's house so let's take advantage of the peace and quiet." Jayme jumped from the passenger side of the SUV. "Let's get you situated and maybe get a head start on a little wine and some cheese and crackers before everyone gets here."

"Sounds like a plan."

This was it. Two days in Texas to plead her case. It wasn't going to change her life, but it was going to give her peace of mind.

CHAPTER 2

Huckleberry "Huck" Duncan couldn't think of anything he hated more than parties. However, everyone from his team was going; these men were more like his brothers than Sawyer had ever been.

While each team he'd been assigned to had become his family, this one felt like home. Like this was where he was destined to land.

These men had truly become his family.

Not the shithead that shared his blood and thought it was okay to beat his wife.

Huck took a hearty swig of his beer and leaned against the fence in Rocket's backyard. Everyone on Rocket's team was married with kids. The majority of his team was on the younger side and while a few had long-term girlfriends, none had tied the knot. Yet.

Though Cannon was engaged. That had happened just as Huck joined the team.

While Huck felt like he belonged with these men, that was on the battlefield. Outside of work, he wasn't so sure. Socializing was something Huck struggled with ever since his mother's death. Of course, it wasn't her dying that had caused his withdrawal. It was everything that lead up to her death and the events that followed that forced Huck to be a guarded man.

Rocket stepped from the sliding glass doors carrying a tray of cheese and crackers. He set it on the table and conversated with a few members of his team. Huck didn't know Rocket that well, but he seemed like a stand-up guy.

However, for the last year, Huck did his best to avoid Rocket. Not because he didn't like the man. He did. Rocket had a wicked sense of humor and had an uncanny ability to keep everyone's spirits up when the shit hit the fan.

But because his wife, Jayme, happened to be Aaliyah's cousin, Huck needed to keep a safe distance.

No one in Texas knew about Aaliyah or his

brother or what happened. He never talked about it and his brother had died before he was transferred to this team. Though, he had to wonder what Rocket and Jayme knew about him and what they thought; however, he'd never ask.

That was his past.

And since no one pressured him about his family, there was no reason to bring it up.

"You have the best resting bitch face of anyone I have ever met," Knox, one of his team members and the best sniper on the base, said.

Of all the men Huck knew, he had to be the closest to Knox for the sole reason that Knox never had a girlfriend. Sure, he dated. But they never lasted and he almost never brought a date to a gathering like this.

"So I've been told." He raised his beer and clanked it against Knox's. "I've never met a group of people who throw so many random parties before."

Knox laughed. "It's just the ones with families. I think they get tired of dealing with kids and need adult company, but I get tired of everyone asking me when I'm going to settle down. What's wrong with wanting to remain single?"

"Nothing, man." Huck had thought that one day he'd have a whole houseful of rug rats. At thirty-five, it wasn't his age that prevented him from marriage and family.

That ship had sailed a year ago.

He couldn't forgive himself for leaving her with that animal he called a brother when she'd needed him the most. Seeing her the next day, battered and bruised and covered in blood, had been too much.

Sawyer had been right about Huck all along.

Huck was a coward.

For months she'd been trying to get ahold of him, wanting to explain. However, how could he tell the only woman he'd ever loved that he knew Sawyer had a reputation for hurting women. That he'd seen it firsthand and while he'd tried to help the woman Sawyer dated before he married Aaliyah, he failed with her too. She stayed until Sawyer had tired of her and found someone else.

Namely, Aaliyah.

When Huck left that night, he wondered if Sawyer might flex his muscles but his pride after being lied to had kept him from checking in on Aaliyah until it had been too late.

There was also the fact that Huck was no saint. He'd done things. Unspeakable things. Before he landed in the Army.

Huck ran a hand across his unshaven face before

taking another swig. His belly soured like it did every time he thought about Aaliyah, which was every fucking day of his life.

She was the first thing he thought of when he woke up and the last thing before he closed his eyes at night.

And when he slept, she haunted his dreams like the ghost of Christmas past.

The only person that Huck ever discussed this with had been a therapist who constantly told him he wasn't his brother's keeper and Aaliyah had chosen to lie to both Huck and Sawyer and she knew the consequences of those lies.

However, the reality was that if Aaliyah hadn't killed Sawyer, he would have killed her first and Huck was honestly thankful she was the one who came out on top.

That, he had no guilt over. Not a single drop.

Just like he had no regrets over killing his mother.

It's what happened after that ate him alive. The constant looking over his shoulder and wondering if this was the day his past was finally going to catch him and put an end to this fake life he'd made for himself.

"Hey, Huck," Rocket called. "Can you come here for a second? I need your help."

"There are how many able-bodied soldiers here and you pick on me," he said with a chuckle. He smacked Knox on the back. "Catch you on the flip side."

"I have no idea why you always say that. You're not a trucker."

"Yeah, but I was raised by one."

"I didn't know that's what your dad did," Knox said.

"My dad was a deadbeat poker player who died when I was ten." Huck left out that it was his brother who killed their father. Sawyer had only been twelve. In the end, it was considered self-defense.

But that wasn't really the case.

And Huck had to live with that truth. Not that his father hadn't had it coming. Because he did. Motherfucker beat him and his brother regularly.

But being murdered in your sleep wasn't self-defense.

It was rare that Huck ever spoke about his family, but when he did, it always came out ass-backwards. Today would be no different and he was feeling especially ornery. "My mom was the trucker. She was one badass bitch. And not in a good way."

She beat the ever-loving crap out of both her boys. She used to tell him and Sawyer that after their father died, it was her duty to take over as the disciplinarian. All they'd done is trade one bastard for another one. She ruled her house with a heavy dose of fear. She resented Sawyer for what he'd done and hated Huck just because he existed. Back then, Sawyer and Huck were as thick as thieves. All they had was each other, but deep down, Huck was absolutely terrified of his big brother. He could see the evil that lurked in his soul and he watched it firsthand when Sawyer brought home his first girlfriend.

Knox tilted his head. "I have to ask what the hell that means."

"Let's just say she dropped me on my head. On purpose." Huck could hear his head crack open and he could feel the searing pain as his mother smashed it with a baseball bat.

Huck had been seventeen years old. He'd had enough. He was sick and tired and he grabbed the first thing he could find.

A butcher knife.

He swung and struck his mother in the neck.

It would have been self-defense. As a grown man, he knew that to be fact. As a scared young man, holding a bloody weapon that took his mother's life, he wasn't so sure. And his older brother, along with a friend of his whose father happened to have loads of money and ties to people Huck never wanted to know, decided it was in Huck's best interest if their mom didn't die the same way their father had. To this day Huck regretted going along with Sawyer's plan but as Gunney, the man who orchestrated the entire thing and helped Huck enlist in the Army said, "What's done is done. Time to live your best life."

That's what Huck had tried to do.

"That sucks," Knox said. "Now I understand why in the last year you've never had family come visit."

"You're my family." Huck nodded. He meant that in the truest sense of the word. Every team he'd bonded with but not quite like this one. These men were special. They were truly his brothers in the ways that counted.

"You better go help Rocket before he comes over here and drags your sorry ass to whatever project he needs you for."

"I swear Logan's team thinks we're their B group."

"We do shadow training with them, so we kind of are." Knox laughed. "I'll hold up the fence for you."

"You're a good man." Huck strolled across the yard. He generally wasn't a party kind of guy. When he wasn't deployed on a mission, he much preferred to stay as busy as possible at the base. When he wasn't working, he'd go hiking, fishing, or stay at home and watch some documentary. Anything to avoid socializing.

It wasn't his thing.

"What's up?" he asked Rocket.

"I need help moving something."

Huck shrugged. Seemed like a weird request and he could have asked anyone, including Oz who stood three feet away. "Sure thing." Huck followed him into the kitchen and through the family room.

He glanced at the walls, which were lined with pictures of his kids.

Adorable little buggers.

Well behaved too.

Rocket and Jayme were picture-perfect parents. Disciplinarians without being over the top. They ruled their house fairly. They expected their children to be respectful of their elders, but also showed them how to express themselves appropriately. The few times Huck met their son Connor, he looked him in the eye and gave him a firm handshake. And the young boy wasn't afraid to speak his mind.

It was obvious to anyone who stepped foot in this house that it was a home filled with love, honor, and kindness.

Something that Huck hadn't experienced as a child.

He rounded the corner and stepped into what appeared to be an office. He paused midstep at the threshold. His jaw slacked open. His chest tightened.

In the middle of the room stood Aaliyah.

All the oxygen in Huck's lungs escaped and he couldn't suck in a breath. Everything around Aaliyah blurred into oblivion. He could only see her and nothing else.

And she looked magnificent with her long dark hair dangling over her shoulders like a cascading waterfall. Her thick lashes blinked over her intense blue eyes. She wore blue jeans that hugged her hips and a loose-fitting blouse that if you asked him was pink in color, but she'd say it was coral or some such nonsense.

He swallowed.

Hard.

Then he cleared his throat, trying to find the courage to spin on his heel and double-time it right to his fucking car.

However, he was frozen in that spot. Unable to move. Or speak.

"I'm sorry to have ambushed you this way," Rocket said. "I'll give the two of you some privacy." He sidestepped Huck, shutting the door behind him, leaving Huck alone with the one woman he had no control around.

This wasn't good.

"What are you doing here?" Huck folded his arms. He gathered up as much anger and hostility as he could. He held on to the rage he felt the second he found out she'd lied. He needed those emotions to get through this or he'd end up taking her into his arms and wrapping them around her, doing all that he could to comfort her in ways he hadn't been able to in the past. He'd apologize for not being there for her when she'd needed him most and tell her that he'd do anything to make it up to her if he could.

But he couldn't afford to do that. He needed to remind himself who he was and where he'd come from because at the end of the day, he wasn't any different than Sawyer or their parents.

Not really.

And he couldn't be with her in the forever kind of way. Not anymore. It wasn't because she'd lied to him about being Sawyer's wife. Sure, that was part of it. However, he had to be honest with himself, something he hadn't done the first time he'd gotten married.

"Obviously I came to talk to you." Aaliyah leaned against the big oak desk situated in the center of the room. She held his gaze, though he could tell it took a fair amount of energy to do so.

Her fingers curled around the edge of the wood and her chest rose up and down as she took in a few exaggerated breaths. In the two short weeks they'd spent together, she'd shown her vulnerability. She'd lacked confidence and self-esteem, and yet she was one of the smartest women he'd ever met. He'd wondered what had happened to her that caused her to question herself so intensely.

The answer revealed itself the second he showed up at his brother's house the day Sawyer returned from Singapore.

"We have nothing to say to one another and I don't appreciate you using my friends to get to me."

"Jayme is my cousin." She squared her shoulders. "Or did you seriously not know that?"

He blew out a puff of air. "Not the point and I thought I made myself perfectly clear when I told you that I didn't want to see you again."

"You did." She held up her hand. "You said a ton

of shit that day, but you never once let me speak. You didn't care to hear a thing I had to say."

"You lied to me. You told me your name was Ann."

"That's my middle name and you're the one who had this weird thing about not telling each other our last names. It was supposed to be a fling."

He laughed. "You knew exactly who I was." He tilted his head. "It's not like my first name is all that common and I know Sawyer mentioned me."

"And I'm to believe that your brother never sent you our wedding pictures or our Christmas picture?"

"Yes," Huck said quickly. "I didn't even know Sawyer got married until three years after it happened because we barely spoke and as I told you while we were holed up in that hotel room, I was only there because a friend of the family had passed and I wanted to tell Sawyer in person because I had promised Gunney I would try to mend fences." Huck had no idea why he explained anything to Aaliyah. He owed her nothing.

Well, maybe that wasn't entirely true.

"Regardless. You never let me tell you what happened after you left that night."

"I don't need you to," he said. "I saw the damage

my brother did and I told you that I was sorry about that. I do feel bad for leaving you alone with him." Huck ran a hand across his head and turned. He looked out the window at all his friends, both single and married, enjoying themselves in the backyard. It became painfully obvious that Jayme and Rocket knew a part of his past that he'd kept close to the cuff.

Nothing he could do about that now.

"I also told the police that you weren't the first woman my brother beat and I signed a statement to that fact." He locked gazes with her and softened his stance, becoming more open. "What you did was self-defense."

"You blamed our affair for Sawyer's death."

Huck nodded. He still did. Had he never slept with Aaliyah, perhaps Sawyer would still be alive, but he didn't give a shit about that. However, Huck would also have to live with the idea that Aaliyah would also then still be trapped in an abusive relationship.

"It's not your fault Sawyer's dead."

"If you think my silence or not wanting to be with you is about blame, then you don't know me at all," Huck said as emotionlessly as he possibly could. "I told you that I value honesty above all else and for two weeks you lied to my face. The moment you realized I was Sawyer's brother, you should have told me you were his wife."

"But I didn't," she interrupted. "And you lied to me as well. You told me that morning that you were leaving, but you didn't. I dropped you at the airport. Kissed you goodbye and everything. Imagine my surprise when you showed up at my doorstep."

He waggled his finger and laughed. "I had every intention of getting on that plane, but Sawyer called." Fuck. Huck didn't want to do this. Not here. Not now. Not ever. "I don't see how reliving this is going to change anything."

"That's where you're wrong," she said. "You need to know why I insisted on taking you to the airport. And I want you to know what happened that night after you left. I need you to know why I lied and it wasn't because I wanted to hurt you or because I was trying to play you or something."

"But you did hurt me and there is no logical reason for you to sleep with your husband's brother," he said behind a clenched jaw. "Especially considering your situation. What did you think was going to happen?" He raised his hand when she opened her mouth to answer. "Please don't answer that."

"That's not fair." She pushed from the desk and planted her hands on her hips. "For the record, I hadn't planned on going to bed with you. I went to your hotel room to beg you for help."

He tossed his head back and laughed. "You begged me all right. But it wasn't to save you." A combination of rage and sadness filled his veins. He would have snuck her out of the city. He had at least three friends within a hundred miles of Manhattan that could have put her in a safe house. He would have done whatever it took to make sure his asshole brother never laid another finger on her beautiful face again.

But she didn't give him the chance.

Fuck it. "Did you think that by having sex with me I'd be beholden to you?"

"No," she said. "You're forgetting who came on to whom."

He opened his mouth, but quickly snapped it shut. "I was nothing but a gentleman," he said softly. "You'd had a lot to drink and I offered you a bed for the night since the hotel was sold out. I did not take advantage of you since nothing happened until you were sober."

"You're missing the point," she said with an exasperated sigh.

"I don't think I am. I'm sorry you had to defend yourself at the hands of my brother's abuse. I only wish you'd found the courage to leave before it came to that."

"That first night, you admitted to me that you didn't have much of a relationship with your brother. You told me that the fact that he couldn't bother to let you know he'd been called away on business when he knew you were coming was one more reason you didn't think you could patch things up with him. I wanted to tell you that you were right. I thought about it but when Sawyer told me he was going to be held up in Singapore even longer, I decided—"

"To seduce me," Huck said, finishing her statement.

"That's not how it happened, but if you need to believe that, then okay. You can have it that way. However, you have to accept that while you might have known your brother was a jerk, you had no clue the kind of man he was."

Huck inched closer. He reached out and palmed her cheek and then quickly dropped his hand to his side as if her skin had burned his hand. "I saw what he did to you and before that, I lived with him for seventeen years. I know exactly who Sawyer was so don't try to tell me I didn't know my own flesh and blood."

A couple of tears dribbled down her face. She lowered her gaze. "You didn't know what he had planned. I had to stop him."

"I told you I don't blame you for what happened to Sawyer. You were in the right for what you did."

"You don't understand," she said softly. "Sawyer was going to—"

"I get it. It was either you or him." Huck needed to end this conversation, considering it was starting to go in circles. He took her chin with his thumb and forefinger. "I've never been angry at you for Sawyer's death. While I don't wish that on anyone, he belonged in prison for what he was doing to you. However, I can't forgive you for lying to me and spending two weeks with me while I told you about my tormented relationship with Sawyer. For me to walk into your home that night and see the two of you play happy couple nearly killed me. I'm glad he's out of your life and I truly hope you can move forward. I want you to be happy. It's just never going to be with me." For good measure, he leaned in and kissed her cheek. "I'm guessing Jayme and Rocket know this history between the two of us, and there's nothing I can do about that. However, I'm hoping it will end there. I'm a private man. I don't talk about—"

"I know and I will respect that. So will they." She tucked her hair behind her ears, turned, and grabbed a large, thick envelope from the desk. "I figured you wouldn't actually hear me out, so this has some key information about what happened that night. I hope you will listen and read." She placed it in his hands. "I can't force you. I can only ask that you'll take the time. I'll be staying here for a few days if you want to talk about what's in there. I promise you that you won't ever hear from me again either way." She squeezed his shoulder and headed for the door.

He stood there, staring at the envelope, wondering what the hell could have happened that would make him change his mind on being lied to.

Nothing.

But bloody fucking hell.

He'd be damned if he could let it go now.

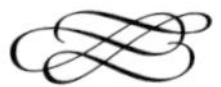

CHAPTER 3

Huck paced in Rocket's office in front of the massive desk. On the back wall was a built-in bookshelf with pictures of Rocket's two kids. Huck paused for a moment and stared at one in particular. The one of Rocket and his son, Connor.

There were no photographs of Huck, his brother, and their father together. Not a single one. Nor were there any fond memories. Only shitty ones, like the time Sawyer had to defend himself.

Only, it wasn't really self-defense.

A lie Huck had told so many times he had started to believe it. However, had he not told it, his dad would have continued to beat the crap out of them and eventually, someone would have died.

Someone always did in the Duncan household.

"Fuck," Huck mumbled. Even in death, Sawyer was still messing with him.

Whatever Aaliyah wanted him to know, she'd gone to great lengths to make sure he had the intel. He might as well hear her out.

Feeling awkward about sitting behind the desk, he eased into the reading chair in the corner. With shaky fingers, he twisted the metal fasteners and opened the envelope. He peered inside, finding a handwritten letter, what appeared to be photographs, and an audio device.

He opted to start with the letter.

Dear Huck,

I'm going to get right to the point. First. I didn't know who you were at first. Huck could have been a nickname for anything. It wasn't until we went to the office to get me my own hotel room because I'd consumed way too much alcohol and you pulled out your credit card to pay for my room.

I saw your name.

I never told you that.

"Nope. You didn't." He sighed. But it made sense because she backed off. A lot. Which made him turn it up.

But I was drunk and I couldn't drive and you insisted that I stay. I have to admit, I was worried at first that maybe you were just like him. But that was a fleeting thought and you bared your soul to me.

Not really. He hadn't told her about their mother or their father or all the horrible things that had been done to both him and Sawyer, or the things they had done throughout their childhood.

But he had expressed his feelings about Gunney. About how Gunney had helped him get into the Army and how he'd promised Gunney on his death bed that he'd tell Sawyer in person about Gunney's death and make an effort to patch things up.

Gunney wasn't a bad man, but he was no saint either. He was the kind of man that lived life in the gray area. He had a code; however, it wasn't one that most law-abiding citizens would agree with. But he was loyal and he wanted Huck to have better. To live life like a normal person and not have to look over his shoulder and wonder the next time he heard a siren if it was meant for him or not.

He wanted the same for Sawyer. It's why he paid for Sawyer's education. Only, Gunney didn't know Sawyer the way Huck did.

Or maybe he did and he was trying to make him a better man.

But nothing could fundamentally change Sawyer.

A few hours into the evening I was conflicted. I

wanted to tell you who I was and I wanted to beg you to help me leave him, and then you kissed me. It was soft and sweet and tender. No one had ever kissed me or held me like that before. I melted in your arms and I got lost in the moment.

I'm not making excuses for my actions. Or maybe I am. And when Sawyer let me know he wasn't coming back for another ten days, I thought I could take the time to think things through, and you and me, we had this deal.

No last names.

I know I was being selfish, but you treated me like I saw how Rocket treats Jayme or how my other friends were treated and I didn't want it to end. That was wrong.

"No shit," he mumbled. But he couldn't blame her for wanting a little piece of happiness and those two weeks were heaven. Even he couldn't deny that.

I figured I'd come clean in the end. I knew you might hate me, and I would take that risk. But I always believed you'd help me leave. However, things changed. What you don't know is that I saw a friend of Sawyer's our last night. And not just any friend. A private investigator. I know now that Sawyer had been home for three days and he knew about us.

Shit. That, Huck didn't know. However, as he thought back to the night he had dinner with Sawyer and Aaliyah at their home, it all made sense. The way

Sawyer had been acting seemed strange. He was being too kind. Too considerate. He behaved as though he and Huck were old friends, which they weren't, and that they shouldn't allow that much time to pass between seeing each other.

It all felt very contrived.

But Huck figured Sawyer was just putting on a good show for his wife. Boy, had he been wrong.

Huck rubbed his temples. He wished he'd brought his beer with him right about now.

When I went home after taking you to the airport, I had every intention of leaving him. I had been saving money. I had a bag packed and a plan. Only, he'd found all that. And he knew about you. He made that abundantly clear when, after you left that night, he showed me the pictures.

"What pictures?" Huck mumbled.

I was mortified. Devastated. And terrified. I had to find a way to warn you, but then I realized that wasn't going to be possible.

Sawyer was going to kill me, and then he was going to frame you for my murder.

He'd told me he'd done this before. That it would be easy to make it look like some love triangle and you came after him blubbering if you couldn't have me, then no one could. I know I panicked. But I also know that Sawyer is capable of some horrible things and destroying you was one of them.

I couldn't let him do that.

So, truth be told, I went at him first. He had to be stopped. Yes. It was me or him. But there was a bigger picture. He told me things about your childhood. About your past. Things that didn't make sense to me at the time. They still don't. But I know Sawyer and he'd find a way to ruin your good reputation.

Over my dead body.

I've shared the pictures he gave me that he took of us, the images the police took along with the police reports and my medical records from that time. I'm also giving you the audio that I managed to tape of the fight. It's gruesome, but I want you to understand what happened and why. The audio isn't about you listening to the horror, but rather the words that were spoken and hearing your brother's plan from his own mouth. Maybe you can make sense of the stories.

I'm sorry that I lied to you. If I had been honest, things would be very different. But we can't go back and change things. We can only move forward with the information we have. Now you have all the facts. Do with them what you want.

Aaliyah.

Fuck. He dropped his head back and stared at the

ceiling. While what she told him wasn't a complete shock, he had been surprised to learn that Sawyer had known all along about the short-lived affair. Especially after a full evening of food and drink. Normally, Sawyer would get cryptic about shit he knew, but not that night. Everything had centered around Gunney and old times and the really weird part had been how attentive Sawyer had been toward his wife.

Huck should have picked up on that as being odd, but instead, he figured it was Sawyer being on his best behavior.

A tap at the door caught his attention.

"Hey. Are you okay?" Rocket stuck his head in. He held out a beer. "I thought you might need one of these."

"I could actually use something stronger."

Rocket pulled a bottle of tequila from behind his back. "This is more of a peace offering for not warning you, but I love my wife and I'd be in the doghouse if I had."

"Now that's what I'm talking about." Huck folded the letter and stuffed it back in the envelope. He'd forgotten he was at a party. He should be outside mingling with his friends, not hiding away in this office. He could listen to the audio and look at all the images in the privacy of his apartment.

Rocket handed the longneck to Huck and set the bottle of tequila on the desk. He stood in front of the small bar and pulled down two glasses before pouring the clear liquid.

Huck clanked his glass with Rocket's and downed half of it. He didn't need to chase it with his beer, it was that smooth. "Wow. That's some serious tequila."

"The best," Rocket said. "It was a gift from Oz. He bought me an entire case last year for Christmas."

"Shit. That's quite the gift."

"Agreed," Rocket said. "I don't mean to pry, but you've been sitting in here for about forty minutes since Aaliyah left. Do you want to talk?"

That was a loaded question and while he hadn't spoken to anyone about this, he wasn't sure he wanted to burden Rocket with it. But Huck didn't know where else to turn. At least Rocket knew some of the history. "Where's Aaliyah?"

"In her room. She and Jayme spoke for a bit and Aaliyah wanted to be alone. She doesn't want us to ignore our friends, so Jayme is popping between being the host to checking in on Aaliyah."

"Is she okay?"

"She seems to be." Rocket leaned back in his chair

and swiveled. "She's worried about you and the fact you haven't left this office."

"What has she told you?" Huck sipped his tequila, even though he wanted to chug the rest of his glass and pour a second. Getting shitfaced to the point he couldn't drive home wouldn't be a good idea. While he knew he was going to have to have a second conversation with Aaliyah, he had no desire to have it happen within the next few hours.

If anything, he wanted at least a day or two for all this information to settle.

"Everything," Rocket said. "Or should I say I assume everything because I can't imagine there's more."

"Oh, trust me, on my end there's a shit ton more and I'm one hundred percent positive she didn't and doesn't know all the skeletons in Sawyer's closet."

"Can I ask you something?"

"Sure," Huck said.

"Did you know everything she told you today?"

"No," Huck admitted. "However, Aaliyah has been under the assumption that I chose not to speak to her because she thought I blamed her for Sawyer's death. That I somehow had a loyalty to him when I didn't and she should have known that from our conversations."

"That's only partly true," Rocket said. "You have to understand that she had every intention on ending Sawyer's life that day. It wasn't premeditated in the legal sense of the word. But the second you walked out that door and he started talking and using his fists, she knew what she had to do."

"I get that," Huck said. "It's still self-defense. Sawyer beat the shit out of her for years. He held her prisoner, for lack of a better word, and a good lawyer would have been able to make her see that."

"Well, she did have an excellent one who was able to make a judge see that, and no charges were ever filed against her."

"I'm glad about that. I've never blamed her for Sawyer's death, and I told her when I saw her the next day that I was sorry for what happened and she did the right thing."

"I know." Rocket nodded. "But she thought she was protecting you. She absolutely believed that Sawyer was going to ruin you by pinning her murder on you."

"I'm sure he had every intention of doing exactly that." Huck took another slow draw of his adult beverage before staring at what little was left of the drink. He'd kept his brothers-in-arms at a safe distance emotionally, even though he considered them the closest thing he'd ever had to a real family. He didn't want to dump this shit on anyone. He'd rather bottle it up and stuff it deep in his soul for safekeeping.

However, Rocket and Jayme knew things and Huck needed to deal with them, for Aaliyah's sake. He did owe her that much.

"Knowing my brother the way I do, he got off on her fear that night, wondering if he knew about us or if he would find out." Huck swallowed the bile that smacked the back of his throat. "I can barely say these words, but he probably raped her on countless occasions."

"I guess you haven't read, seen, or heard everything in that packet."

"Fuck," Huck muttered as he stood. He set his drink on the desk and stomped to the window. His gut soured. That thought had creeped into his mind once or twice and each time he pushed it out so fast he barely had time to process the information. He had so many mixed emotions about knowing the truth. He wanted to reach into his brother's grave and strangle the man with his bare hands.

He needed to find Aaliyah and wrap his arms around her and hold her close, letting her know that someone loved and valued her the way she deserved. Only, that could never be him.

He'd failed her more than once.

"She doesn't blame you for anything that happened," Rocket said.

Huck turned. "She should. I could have taken her with me. I could have called my brother out on his bad behavior."

"But you didn't know."

"There's a reason my brother and I stopped speaking to each other and it's because he was an asshole." Huck ran his finger across the desk before pointing to the bottle of tequila. "So, I knew."

Rocket nodded. "Perhaps, but you couldn't have predicted the outcome of that night."

Huck poured a full glass. It might be a while before he headed home. "About eleven years ago, before my brother moved to Singapore, he was dating this woman. Real nice girl. He put her in the hospital a couple of times. The last time it happened she was able to get away from him, thankfully. But he was done with her anyway since he'd met Aaliyah."

"She wasn't your fault either."

"I understand that," Huck said. "However, the second I stepped foot into my brother's home and I saw Aaliyah, I knew and I left anyway. I let my anger over her lies consume me when I should have been offering her an exit strategy."

"She wouldn't have taken it. Not that night. Not considering what Sawyer had in store for you and the time he had to plan it."

Huck took another long draw of his beverage. It was so smooth he couldn't believe he was drinking alcohol, except his muscles had relaxed and his mind had a certain fogginess to it that it hadn't an hour ago. "She went to that bar with every intention of finding someone to help her leave Sawyer. I don't understand her logic about not telling me and going home to him, but we can't rewrite history, now can we."

"No," Rocket said from his perch behind his big desk. "What I don't understand is why you wouldn't ever hear her side of the story."

"During my short affair with Aaliyah, I told her something that I've never told anyone. Something that has shaped who I am when it comes to relationships with women."

"You actually have those? Because in the year I've known you, I think I've seen you go out on maybe two dates."

Huck cracked a slight smile. Not because he was

proud. No. It was more of a nervous one. "Sawyer was my only living family and we all but parted ways after our mother died."

"I'm sorry for your loss."

Huck wanted to tell his buddy that it was no loss at all, but why open that can of worms. This next juicy piece of information was going to give Rocket and everyone else something to chew on for a long time. "Sawyer went off to college and I joined the Army. We didn't speak much and that was fine. He did his thing and I did mine. When I was twenty-one, I met this girl and I thought I was in love so I got married."

"You're married?" Rocket asked with an arched brow. "To whom? For how long? And what happened?"

"Her name was Gabby. It lasted all of two years and she slept with some guy down the street."

"That sucks."

Huck shrugged. "They are happily married with three kids. Who am I to stand in their way. She and I weren't meant to be."

"You're a good man to have that kind of attitude."

"Trust me. It took a while for me to get here." He eased back into the chair in the corner and stared out the window. "I didn't know about the affair until

Gabby gave birth to a little girl who needed a blood transfusion and I wasn't a match. Turns out, I wasn't her father. But some dude down the street named Jeff was."

"Jesus. That's a shitty-ass story."

"It sure is and I told it to Aaliyah. I could tell she was a woman with a past and all I asked was that she wasn't married or involved with someone. She emphatically denied it. She looked me in the eye and lied. I lived with Gabby, whom I loved, and she lied to me for over a year and I had no idea. I told Aaliyah how that nearly destroyed me and that I didn't believe I could ever recover from that kind of betrayal."

"I understand where you're coming from, I really do," Rocket said. "But seriously, you came up with this no last name thing for a two-week fling where you were going to walk away and never see each other again."

Huck opened his mouth, but Rocket raised his hand, palm out.

"Don't try to backpedal and tell me that you were going to change your mind at the end because you didn't."

"Actually, I did." Huck shifted in his seat. "I guess Aaliyah left out the part where I stuffed a note in her purse with all my contact information and told her that I was sorry for the game and that I cared about her and wanted to get to know her better."

"No. She didn't leave that out," Rocket said. "She didn't find it until after Sawyer was dead. And for the record, that was a stupid way to express your feelings. You should have done it face-to-face."

"Hindsight is perfect vision."

"True statement," Rocket said.

"How long have you known all this about me?"

"Since it happened," Rocket admitted.

"I've been in Texas now for three months. Why did it take her so long to get here?" Seemed like an odd question to ask, but he wanted to know the answer.

"I didn't think she should come during your training with your new team, and then you were on a mission and needed some downtime," Rocket said. "I want you to know that I wasn't on board totally with ambushing you, but considering you wouldn't take her calls and returned every letter, and I did agree that you should at least hear her out—"

"It's fine." Huck waved his hand. He had no fight in him to be angry at Rocket or Jayme for helping to orchestrate any of this. In the end, they were right. He should have listened to Aaliyah's story a long time ago. However, remembering all the excuses and various reasons for his ex-wife's endless lies about why she hadn't told him about the possibility he wasn't the father clung so thick to his heart and soul he couldn't see straight. "If you had warned me, I would have run."

"At least you can be honest about that."

Huck held up the envelope. "You mentioned you know everything. Have you listened to what happened the night my brother died? Looked at the photographs that she's sharing with me?"

"I have not, nor has my wife. Aaliyah said besides it being disturbing, there is private family information that she doesn't believe you'd want people to know." Rocket leaned forward, resting his hands on the desk. "The key component here is that had she not been able to defend herself that night, he would have killed her and he would have had proof that you had an affair with her and it's possible he could have framed you for it."

"Not to mention I went to the bar and got shitfaced." A reality that made Huck cringe. He'd passed out in his room by midnight. Sawyer could have easily come at him while he slept.

However, his curiosity was even more piqued as

to what Sawyer might have said during his fight that night with Aaliyah.

"I have to ask. What are you going to do now?" Rocket asked.

"Well, I've had too much to drink to drive home. So, I guess I'm going to hang here for a bit, if that's okay, and maybe take Aaliyah for a walk."

"You're welcome to stay as long as you need. Aaliyah is in the bedroom at the end of the hallway."

Huck jumped to his feet, tucking the envelope under his arm. "No time like the present."

CHAPTER 4

"The party is winding down," Jayme said as she stood in the doorway. "Let me know if you need anything."

"I will." Aaliyah sat on the bed, leaning against the headboard, hugging one of the big fluffy pillows. "I think I'm just going to take a bath and go to bed."

"Huck hasn't left. His pickup is still parked out front."

"It's been almost two hours. If he wanted to talk, he would have come found me by now." Aaliyah had done exactly what she had wanted. She spoke her peace. She gave Huck the missing information that he hadn't been privy to. That's all she needed. If Huck didn't ever want to speak to her again, she could live with that.

What she couldn't live with was knowing that his

brother had known about the affair and had been playing his brother for a fool that night at dinner and then planned on framing him for her murder.

But that wasn't even the worst part.

It was ruining Huck's good name that twisted her gut, especially if anything on that audio recording was true.

"All right," Jayme said. "If you need me, don't hesitate to come find me." She gently closed the door.

Aaliyah let out a long sigh and tossed the pillow to the other side of the bed. She padded across the room and into the bathroom. She sat on the edge of the tub and twisted the handle when a tap at the door caught her attention. "What did you forget?" She stepped back into the bedroom and froze. Her heart caught in her throat. She couldn't breathe, even if she tried.

"Hey," Huck said. "Can I come in?"

"Yeah. Sure." She glanced around. The only place to sit was on the bed. She chose the corner.

He leaned against the door after he closed it. He set the envelope on the dresser. "I read the letter, but I haven't had a chance to look at the pictures or listen to the audio."

She sucked in a deep breath, doing her best not

to allow anger to rise to the surface. That wouldn't help the situation. "Why not?"

"I was interrupted before I had the chance, and then I decided maybe we should talk more."

"Oh. I see."

"Is there water running in the bathroom?"

"Shit." She'd completely forgotten about the bathtub. Quickly, she turned off the faucet. When she returned to the bedroom, Huck had made himself comfortable on the bed.

Wonderful.

Well, she wasn't going to stand there awkwardly. She found a spot, snagged a pillow, and hugged it for dear life. "I'm listening," she said.

"I have questions."

"Okay."

"Besides hitting you that night. Did my brother… did he… did he…"

"You want to know if Sawyer raped me," she said with as little emotion as she could manage.

"Yes."

She swiped at her cheeks. It always amazed her how easily the tears came. She nodded, unable to answer with words.

"I'm sorry."

"It wasn't the first time. I can't say that the last few years of our marriage was consensual."

"That doesn't make me feel any better." Huck took her hand and squeezed. He ran his thumb over the top and he smiled sweetly, like he'd done so many times during their short-lived affair. "Why did you stay with him?"

"That's a fucking loaded question." One she struggled to answer, but only because it didn't logically or rationally make sense. "When I met Sawyer, I was a successful salesperson. I was young and I thought I oozed confidence. If you ask Jayme, I was a self-centered little bitch who only cared about herself and that would be a true statement."

"What happened?"

"Sawyer happened."

"I guess that's a fair statement."

"He could be charming and he'd sweep a girl off her feet. The first two years we were together he only hit me twice."

"Only?" Huck lowered his chin.

She chuckled. "That's how you justify it to yourself. All his jealous behavior and the way he treated me was because he loved me. When we moved back to the States and got married, everything changed. But even that didn't happen overnight, and by the time I left my job, I was too ashamed to ask anyone for help. I was a shell of the person I used to be, and Sawyer controlled every aspect of my life."

"He was good at that. He did that to me when we were kids, especially after our dad died," Huck said. "That brings me to another question. What's on this audio that you want me to hear?"

"Sawyer told me about how you'd both gotten away with murder before and that he knew how to do it." She turned, sitting cross-legged. She fiddled with the corners of the pillow. "He said you killed your mother. I didn't believe him, of course, but the way he talked about the specifics of his plan and how he was going to take me to the hotel you were staying at and stage—"

Huck pressed his index finger against her quivering lips. "You have all that on audio?"

She nodded.

"Who else has listened to it?"

"No one," she said. "Why?"

"You didn't give it to the police?"

She shook her head.

Huck slipped from the bed and paced at the foot. He ran a hand across the top of his head. "Why not?

Didn't they need to listen to it for evidence or something?"

"I didn't even know I had recorded it on my phone until a few days later and no. They had enough to rule it self-defense." She sat up taller. "You're scaring me."

Huck took the envelope and shook it. "Is this the only recording?"

"Yes. Why?"

"I'm going to destroy it and I'm going to ask you to never speak of it again. Can you do that for me?"

She clutched the feather pendant her memaw had given her for her sweet sixteen. Her heart beat so fast she thought it was going to jump right out of her chest. "Is there any truth to what Sawyer was saying?"

"I'm sure my brother told a sick, twisted version of what really happened. He enjoyed doing shit like that to fuck with people."

She gasped and covered her mouth. Sawyer had told her so many things that night.

Things that about how he'd killed his father, and even though it had been ruled self-defense, it wasn't.

There were other confessions too and many implicated Huck, making him look like a common criminal, which was how Sawyer was going to be able to nail his ass—his words, not hers.

"No. Please tell me Sawyer was lying. That's not who you are. You're not like him."

"You're right. I'm nothing like my brother. Not even close. But I can't allow this kind of recording to exist. If the authorities were to ever hear it, they could open an investigation and that would be bad for me. Very bad," he said with wide eyes. "Can you promise me you'll never speak of this to anyone? Ever."

"Yes," she said softly.

"Thank you." He turned and gripped the door handle.

"Huck."

"What?" He glanced over his shoulder.

"Did you?"

"My mother and Sawyer were cut from the same cloth," he said. "Let's just say it was me or her."

Aaliyah sat there with her mouth gaping open. She couldn't believe her ears. Sawyer had been sort of telling her the truth, though Huck was right. His brother had put his own sick twist on reality.

Shit. She couldn't let Huck leave this way.

"Huck. Wait." She raced out of the bedroom, through the family room, and out the front door, finally catching him at his truck. She curled her fingers around his biceps.

"It's ironic that you didn't believe him when he was telling the truth," Huck said, jerking his arm free.

"He was manipulating me and I wasn't falling for it. He wanted me to think you were a bad man and you're not. If it was self-defense, you did nothing wrong."

"Only, someone else served time for my mother's death. Granted, that person was convicted of five other murders, so they were going to prison anyway, but that's not the point. We covered it up. My entire life is a sham." He waved his hand toward the house. "I don't belong with these men. I don't deserve the kind of respect that they have." He laughed, though it wasn't a funny kind of laugh. More of a dark, morbid laugh. "Perhaps I wouldn't have gone to prison for what happened with my mother. But I should have for what I did after. And then there are the things that happened before that. The things that Sawyer had me do."

"You were a child," Aaliyah pleaded with Huck. "It was an abusive situation. First your father, then Sawyer and your mother. Don't you see? It's not that much different than what I was dealing with, only worse because you were a kid. You didn't know any better."

"Oh yes, I did," he said. "I just wanted out and Gunney offered me exactly that and I took it."

She palmed his cheek. "You're a good man and you deserve to be here."

"No. I don't." He let out a long breath. "My re-enlistment papers are sitting on my desk. I was going to turn them in this week, but I realize it's time to end this charade. I've got six months left, and then I'm out." He opened the driver's side door. "Thanks for reminding me who I really am."

She took a step as the truck lurched forward.

"Is everything okay?" Rocket asked as he approached.

"No," Aaliyah said. "I need to borrow your car."

"What happened?"

"Even dead, Sawyer is fucking up my life."

CHAPTER 5

Huck hit the play button again. His head pounded faster than his heart beat. Fuck. Why did he keep playing this tape? He thought he'd put the past behind him and he believed he'd come to terms with what he'd done. Gunney had made it perfectly clear that there was no turning back time. That he couldn't confess his sins. Sawyer had made sure of that because if Huck did, he sure as shit would go to prison.

Huck killed our mother.

Murdered her right in front of me. In cold blood. While she slept.

I had to get Gunney and we had to cover it up so Huck wouldn't go to prison. That's where he belongs. Prison.

Right there was where Sawyer hit Aaliyah. Huck could still hear one of her bones crack.

Or break.

He shivered as he stopped the tape. He couldn't listen to it again.

Gunney had done his best to make sure Huck turned his life around. He'd done the same for Sawyer, but Sawyer took Gunney's gift and used it to con people into believing he was a good person.

Fuck. Huck had some serious apologizing to do. He had no right treating Aaliyah the way he had. She'd been nothing but respectful when it came to his privacy. So what that she'd taken the news he'd killed his mother in self-defense with a gasp and a look of shock.

That was a normal response to that kind of news.

The only real question he had for himself was if he'd re-enlist. Up until being assigned to this team, he'd felt like a fraud. But not anymore. However, being reminded of where he'd come from and what he'd done only made him wonder what his fellow Delta Force team members would think of him if they found out.

Someone pounded at the door. He glanced at his watch. It was only nine in the evening. Not horribly late, but no one ever stopped by at this hour. He stood and meandered toward the door. He glanced through the peephole.

Aaliyah.

She saved him the trip to apologize in the morning.

He pulled open the door and turned. "Want something to drink?" He didn't bother to glance over his shoulder. He just went straight for the mini bar next to the small galley kitchen in his tiny one-bedroom apartment. He took two wineglasses and poured from his favorite bottle of red, which he knew she'd like. He searched his brain for the right words. He so sucked at this kind of stuff. His ex-wife had made sure he'd have trust issues for the rest of his life.

Of course, what happened with Aaliyah hadn't helped. But that was an entirely different story.

"You're not going to kick me out," she said as more of a statement than a question, which he found amusing.

"You came all this way to say something to me and I've learned you don't give up that easily." He handed her a glass and then sat back down on the sofa.

She joined him on the other end, curling her feet

up under her butt. She pointed at the audio device. "You haven't destroyed it yet."

"I ended up listening to some of it."

"Why?"

"I have no fucking clue," he said. "If I could raise my brother from the dead and kill him all over again, I'd do it."

"Can't say I blame you for that thought." She raised her glass. "He was a prick."

"For the record, the story he tells on how our mother died, is how he killed our father. Though, not that I want to ever defend Sawyer, our dad wasn't any better than our mom. It was a shitty childhood all around. If a week went by without one of us getting a black eye, it was a hell of a good week. The difference, though, was that Sawyer became like them."

"I'm glad you can see the difference."

He'd always understood he wasn't like the rest of his family, but sometimes the guilt over what he'd done ate him alive from the inside out. "The fact that I could walk away from you knowing that Sawyer was going to lay his hands on you, makes me no better."

"Oh, my God. Fucking stop with that shit." She glared at him with daggers shooting from her eyes as if they were machine guns. "Sawyer wasn't going to let you stay, and you knew that. He practically shoved you out the door."

"I suppose that's true." Huck rubbed the back of his neck.

"I'm sorry I reacted the way I did. I believed Sawyer was fucking with me."

"But you knew enough not to share that audio recording with anyone or tell even Rocket about it, though you certainly shared a lot of other information with him and Jayme."

"They knew about Sawyer. Hell, Jayme even met him. I had to tell them that part, but the rest wasn't my business to tell anyone. You might think I'm a lying, two-faced bitch, but—"

"I don't think that." He took her wineglass and set both down on the coffee table. "Considering the things I've done in my past, I should have been more understanding and I shouldn't have treated you the way I have this past year." He tucked a few pieces of hair behind her ears. "Tell me what you've been up to."

She smiled. "I moved, for one."

"Where to?"

"Upstate for now," she said. "It's temporary while

I look for a job, but I couldn't stand living in the city a second longer."

"I don't blame you there. I hate big cities. What kind of job are you looking for?" It felt good to let all the heavy stuff go and just talk. He'd forgotten how much he enjoyed being with her and listening to her voice, and right now, he didn't want that to end. So, he'd keep asking questions until she said it was time to go.

Only all he could think about was kissing her and that was something he didn't think would be a good idea. If he started, he wouldn't want to stop.

"I don't want to go back to sales, so I was thinking a behind-the-scenes job. Maybe data analyst or something. I'm good with numbers. But I've been out of the workforce for a few years so it might take some time."

"Do you have a headhunter helping you?"

"I do."

"And where ideally would you like to live —work?"

"Anywhere but New York," she said with a nervous laugh.

"Would you consider Texas?" Why the fuck would he ask that? It wasn't like he wanted to get involved, but she did have family here and it was her hometown, so it made sense.

"Absolutely. But who knows where I'll find the right job."

"You're smart. You'll find something." He stared at her for a long moment, unsure of what to ask next. He'd had so many questions pop into his mind ten minutes ago, but now his brain was blank, except for a bunch of thoughts that he was too terrified to entertain.

But only because if he did, there would be no turning back this time. There wouldn't be any games. They knew each other's deepest, darkest secrets. There was no past to be afraid of. No lies to be hidden. No skeletons to fall out of the closet. Only two people who were attracted to each other.

She licked her plump rosy lips.

He wanted to taste them once again. Leaning closer, he could no longer resist the urge. When his mouth met hers, heat crawled across his skin like flames taking to a log.

Their tongues collided in a familiar dance. It was wet, wild, and wicked.

Heat filled every muscle in his body and desire consumed his soul.

He lifted her off the couch and effortlessly

carried her into his bedroom. Tugging at her clothing, he removed every stitch until she stood before him, gloriously naked. The moonlight shone through the window, casting a glow over her porcelain skin, showing every womanly curve.

"You're even more beautiful than I remember." He traced a path from her belly button to her breasts with his index fingers.

Her skin broke out in tiny goosebumps. Carefully, he pushed her to the bed.

She stared with wide, eager eyes as he slowly undressed. "Let me help with that." She sat up and pushed his hand from his zipper.

"I'm not going to argue with you."

"Good."

He held his breath, preparing for what was about to come next as he stepped from his jeans. In the past, she'd been tentative and that's what he liked.

And she didn't disappoint as she brought him to her mouth, kissing softly. Tenderly.

He pooled her hair on top of her head. He wouldn't be able to stand this too long without losing control and that was something he could never do with Aaliyah.

Never.

"Come here," he whispered.

She glanced up and smiled.

He pressed his index finger under her chin and guided her to his lips. "You're an amazing woman. Don't let anyone ever tell you otherwise."

"Do you know you said that to me the first time we were together?"

"I know. I remember." He chuckled. "I could tell that someone had made you feel less than and that bothered me. I wanted you to feel special."

"I did," she said. "I remind myself of that all the time."

"I'm glad." He took her in his arms and lay her next to him in the bed.

She moaned as he took her nipple into his mouth. All he wanted in this moment was to bring her pleasure. That's all that mattered. He made sure he hit every erogenous zone. He listened to the intensity of her moans. He studied the movement of her body and responded with earnest. Whatever she demanded, he would give.

"Yes," she whispered in his ear as she dug her nails into his back. "I need you."

He didn't hold back. He caved to both of their desires. Her climax filled him like the ocean crashing on shore. His came only seconds later, colliding with hers as if they were ships passing in the night.

It was a while before his breath became normal again. He rolled to his side and pulled the covers over their bodies. He pulled her close and kissed her temple. "You don't have to leave, do you?"

"Are you asking me to spend the night?"

He chuckled. "Yeah. I am."

"I think I'd like to stay."

"Good," he said. "Not to bring up a sore subject, but I haven't looked at the pictures or anything else in that envelope, like your records. Is there anything else I need to know?"

Her body stiffened.

"What is it?" he asked.

"Can we talk about this in the morning?"

"Is it bad?"

She tilted her head and caught his gaze. "It's just sad."

"Okay. In the morning it is." He closed his eyes and for the first time in the last year, he wasn't haunted by what-ifs.

CHAPTER 6

Aaliyah propped her head up and watched as Huck lay blissfully asleep. She wondered if the man dreamed and if so, what it was about. He looked so damn peaceful she hoped it was something nice. Maybe something about her.

Perhaps that was too much to ask.

She bit down on her fingernail. He'd asked her to spend the night. But that didn't mean anything. He'd told her after his divorce, he wasn't the kind of guy who asked a woman to leave right after sex. He believed that to be disrespectful and he would never treat anyone that way. Even though he didn't want a long-term relationship or to ever get married again, he still enjoyed companionship. He struggled with trust. It was something he wanted to overcome and he worked at it.

Something his note that he stuffed in her purse told her and the fact that he wanted to get to know her better showed he'd begun to trust her, which she hadn't deserved. Not back then.

So what did all this mean now? Was this closure? Did he want to start something up with her? Did she?

Yes. One hundred percent yes. She loved him with everything she was and that was never going to change. But she was in New York, and he lived in Texas. Packing up and moving without a job wouldn't be smart.

Not that she had a job now, but it didn't feel right, even though Jayme and Rocket had been trying to get her to move for the last few months. However, now that Huck was living in Killeen, it seemed like it would be too much if she came home. He might think she was expecting too much and it might make things worse just as they were making progress.

He blinked.

"I can feel you staring at me," he whispered. His fingers tickled up her spine. "How long have you been awake?"

"Just a few minutes."

"What time is it?"

"Seven."

He brushed his lips over hers in a warm kiss. "I haven't slept that late in a long time."

"I was kind of woken up by a text from Jayme. They will be coming over by nine to get their vehicle. Rocket has some errands to run with Connor and Jayme has to take Kayleigh somewhere."

"The joys of parenthood."

She'd wanted to be a mother. When she'd first met and married Sawyer, they'd had the perfect plan for children. However, no way would she bring a child into that marriage. She did everything she could, short of sterilization, to prevent pregnancy.

Yet it still happened, only Sawyer hadn't been the father and she lost the baby anyway.

She should be glad that Huck returned the first few letters. She'd broken down and told him about his child. She had to because she thought that was the only way he'd speak to her. It wasn't to trap him into anything. But she knew he'd want to know.

"What are you so deep in thought over?"

She put on a smile. She was not going to tell him right this second. She needed a cup of coffee before that conversation. However, she did have other questions. "I'm not sure how to even bring any of this up."

He fluffed his pillow and sat up, pulling her with him, wrapping his arms around her body. He ran his hand up and down her skin. "Whatever's on your mind, just say it."

"What does last night and holding me now mean?"

He kissed her forehead. "What do you want it to mean?"

"Oh no. You can't answer my question with another one. That's not fair."

He chuckled. "I honestly haven't a clue," he said. "How long are you here for?"

She glanced up at him with a narrowed stare. "So another fling?"

"I didn't necessarily say that, but we don't know each other and you live in New York, and not only do I live in Texas, but my ass is owned by the government. They say jump, I don't even ask how high. I just jump. And while I'm stateside right now, my phone could ring and I could be deployed tomorrow. Being involved with me would be like being involved with a whack-a-mole."

She laughed. "That is the dumbest analogy I've ever heard."

"It's the only one I've got, and you haven't answered my question."

"I planned on staying a couple of days to a week. Unless things went really shitty, and then I told Jayme that I'd be on the next plane back to New York."

"I do have to work on base all week, but why don't we try getting to know one another the right way this time."

"What do you mean, exactly?" She pulled the sheet around her body and sat up.

"Dating. Of course, you can stay here if you want. That's entirely up to you. I thought today we could drive down to Stillhouse Hollow Lake and rent a boat. Grab a bite to eat for dinner somewhere and tomorrow we can do something else."

"Sounds like a great day." She dropped the sheet and tugged the comforter, exposing the rest of his body. "However, it's missing one key element." She straddled him, taking him slowly.

He groaned, gripping her hips. "I can't imagine a better way to start my morning." He took her nipple into his mouth and tortured it with his masterful tongue. She'd forgotten what it had been liked to be loved by a man. Sawyer had destroyed that, until Huck came along. He showed her that she deserved to be fulfilled. Desired. That her wants and needs were as important as any man's. The confidence she felt when she was with Huck came naturally. There was no shame in her sexuality. No fear of rejection. Her only concern was that she pleased him as much as he did her.

She rolled her hips and arched her back, taking what she needed. His fingers dug into her thighs. He thrust upward, matching her motions. His thumb touched her intimately, rubbing gently in a circular motion. Dropping forward with her hands on his shoulders, her orgasm tore through her body. It began at her toes, curling them. It moved up her calf muscles, twisting and tightening. Her stomach fluttered. She convulsed uncontrollably as she called out his name.

He swelled inside her, exploding with great force. He took her mouth in a hot, wild kiss. With his hands holding their bodies still, she collapsed on top of him and tried to take a deep breath. It would be a good ten minutes before that would become a possibility.

His hands roamed up and down her back. He kissed her cheek, her neck, and the soft spot under her lobe. "I could use some coffee after that. How about you?"

She laughed. "And food. I'm famished."

"Eggs. Pancakes. Or French toast?"

"French toast, please."

"Why don't you go shower while I make us some grub and call the marina to make sure we can get a boat."

"Sounds like a plan," she said. Butterflies filled her stomach. She had a few expectations when she'd gotten on that plane to Killeen. The first had been Huck wouldn't listen, but that he'd take the time to read her letter and look at the contents of the envelope.

The second had been that maybe they'd talk.

But this?

No. She had not expected he'd want to spend a week with her to see if there was anything there. Well, she knew there was because she was still in love with him, only she wasn't going to tell him that.

Not yet anyway.

One thing at a time and there was one more confession.

After her shower.

* * *

Huck put the last dish in the dishwasher and poured a fresh cup of coffee. He stared out the kitchen window. Jayme and Aaliyah were standing in the driveway, chatting away, all smiles while Rocket and the kids hung in the background, kicking a ball around. Huck had lost his ever-loving fucking mind. What the hell was he thinking by giving this a week? Like that would change anything.

She was still his brother's wife. It didn't matter that Sawyer was dead. It didn't even matter that Huck honestly believed he was in love with Aaliyah and had been since she dropped him off at the airport a year ago.

Love didn't make a relationship.

He still had trust issues and would never marry again. His heart couldn't stand the risk. Even thinking about it made his pulse soar, and not in a good way. It gave him heartburn.

And Aaliyah had lied to him before. Of course, those circumstances were special and he couldn't blame her, not really. He had his own game of no last names, and she hadn't been the first woman he'd done that with. It was his way of weeding out the crazy.

It was truly stupid.

He turned and headed toward the front door

when he eyed the envelope. There was something else in there she wanted to talk about. Something that made her sad. He set his mug down and pulled out the images of him and Aaliyah from a year ago. He'd glanced at some of them last night. His brother's private investigator had done a thorough job of capturing the affair. The only thing left were her medical records, only they weren't from the day of the murder. No. They were from two months later.

Pregnant.

Miscarriage.

"What the fuck?" He reread the reports. And then he studied the dates.

The front door opened.

"Jayme and Rocket are leaving. Do you want to say goodbye?" Aaliyah smiled at him as if there was nothing wrong. Like another betrayal wouldn't destroy any chance they had.

His heart dropped to his stomach. He waved the papers. "You thought this could wait?"

Her smile faded. "Yes. I did."

"I think it's best if you go with them."

"Excuse me?" She glanced over her shoulder. "No. We're talking this out now."

"Was I the father?"

"Yes," she admitted.

"And you didn't think I should know?"

"Are you fucking kidding me?" She slammed the door shut and closed the gap.

He took a step back.

She poked him in the chest. "I wrote you letters telling you about the baby before I had a miscarriage. You returned them. Unopened. So, you don't get to be this upset that I decided to wait another day to tell you about something that doesn't exist." She wiped the tears that dribbled down her face. "I went through that miscarriage alone. There was no one there to hold my hand. No one to tell me it was going to be okay. Not a single person, so you can take your hurt feelings and shove them right up your ass. You lost the right to be mad at me the day you chose to fucking ignore me."

He guessed he deserved that one.

"Maybe so, but when this came up yesterday, you should have told me. This is a big deal."

"I know. I lived it." She tugged at her hair, pulling it over her shoulder and twisting it.

He hadn't used a condom. "Shit," he mumbled. "Are you taking birth control pills?"

"Yes," she said. "I don't want to go through that hell again." She turned on her heel and left, leaving him wondering if she meant being pregnant had been hell, or just the miscarriage.

Or both.

Fuck.

He didn't know a thing about women.

He bolted through the front door. "Aaliyah, wait."

"No." She gripped the passenger side of Jayme's minivan. "I'm done with the Huck roller-coaster ride. We know everything there is to know about each other and we're not a good fit. For the record, that was the last piece of information that I needed to tell you. And just so we're clear, I wanted you to know about the baby. Not because I wanted to hurt you or because I was trying to keep something from you. It was actually the complete opposite. I know how important honesty is to you and that's what I was trying to be, but you threw it in my face because you're nothing more than a small child who lives with a lot of pain from the past. I'm sorry about what your ex-wife did to you. That's shitty. And I'm sorry about all the horrible things Sawyer and your parents did. No person should live through that. Hell, no one should experience the things I did. But guess what, I'm not going to be a prisoner to it anymore. I hope you find peace, Huck. I really do." She climbed into Jayme's vehicle.

Jayme waved as they drove away.

Rocket, on the other hand, didn't leave. "Are you okay?"

Huck nodded. Aaliyah was right. Every single fucking word. He needed to get his head on straight before he tried to fix things. "Can you do me a favor?"

"Sure."

"Don't let her fly back to New York in the next couple of days."

"Did you just really piss her off that much?"

"You have no idea," Huck mumbled. "It might take a miracle for her to forgive me."

"Why don't you go after her now?"

"She needs a day to cool off. I need a day to get my jumbled thoughts in the right place. The one thing I know about Aaliyah is when she's hurt to her core, it's not about the apology, it's about the action. I'm just not sure either one of us is ready for that."

"That's the most cryptic thing I've ever heard."

Huck laughed. "All that matters is I know what it means. Just don't let her leave. I'll be by tomorrow, if that's okay."

"Sure thing."

Well, Huck didn't do things small. Why should this be any different?

CHAPTER 7

Needing a different perspective from someone who didn't know the history, Huck called his buddy Cannon.

"I'm glad Jolene didn't mind you coming fishing with me today." Huck dropped his line. The fish weren't biting much, but no matter. Sometimes it wasn't about what you caught, but about being out on the water. This gave Huck all the time in the world to consider his next move. It had to be the right one. He couldn't fuck this up. If he came on too strong, he'd lose her. Not strong enough, same thing.

"Her editor sent her notes on a proposal she's working on for her next book. She was happy to get rid of me for the day."

"You two seem to have a great relationship."

Huck snagged a seltzer from the cooler. He cracked it open and took a swig. Lifting his feet, he rested them on the side of the boat, which rocked gently back and forth in the waves.

"We have our share of ups and downs."

"Can I ask you a couple of personal questions?"

"Does this have something to do with the woman staying at Rocket's place?" Cannon asked. "You disappeared from the party yesterday and we all saw you and her in the front yard."

"It does." Huck reached into his lunch pail and pulled out a turkey sandwich he'd made before leaving the house. He'd made two, one for him and one for Aaliyah. He sucked in a deep breath, enjoying the warm air. He wasn't going to get into all the details from the past, his brother, and all the bullshit. That's not what this was about. Not at the end of the day. "She and I had a thing about a year ago."

"What happened?"

"It's a long, complicated story. We were able to talk through most of it, but then I went and put my foot in my mouth. Now she's pissed and with good reason."

"So why are you here with me instead of trying to make it right with her?"

"We both need some space," Huck said. "But mostly I'm not sure about how I feel and if it's real."

"What do you mean by that?" Cannon shifted, setting his pole in the rod holder. "There's nothing fake about emotions. Whatever you're feeling, it's real."

"Even if they are confusing and conflicting."

"Especially then," Cannon said. "You really care about this woman?"

"Her name's Aaliyah and yes. However, I didn't expect for it to be so intense. I thought that over this past year I'd be able to forget about her, but that never happened. The second I saw her at Rocket's party, it was like we hadn't spent the last year apart. Only the really crazy thing is that we only spent about two weeks together." Huck adjusted the line on his pole as it wiggled with a possible nibble of a fish.

Nope. Just the waves tugging at it.

"I fell hard and fast for Jolene."

"That's what I wanted to ask you about." Huck had no idea why he was so uncomfortable. This shouldn't be that awkward of a conversation. However, he didn't like to be vulnerable. Not like this. And certainly not with his brothers-in-arms. He'd managed to keep his past life locked up in a private vault where no one in the present could touch it. He liked it that way, but now it was all muddled and he had to find a way to come to terms with that fact.

"You want to talk to me about my relationship with my fiancée?"

"More about if you believed in love at first sight before it happened to you."

"Are you questioning if you love Aaliyah or not?"

Love was a strong word and Huck wasn't ready to use it. Not to himself and sure as shit not out loud. But he knew he had to have a handle on his heart before he spoke to Aaliyah again. He needed to know what he wanted.

What he needed.

And more importantly what he could offer. That was the key. He had to be willing to be all in or it wasn't worth it.

For either one of them.

"Let me ask you this," Cannon said. "Does she love you?"

"I have no idea," Huck admitted. "Before I fucked everything up, we were going to spend time together, getting reacquainted. In my mind, that was a formality because I thought I'd end up scaring her away if I told her what I was really thinking and feeling."

"And what's that, exactly?"

"I want her to move here. She's not working right now, currently looking for a job, anywhere in the country except New York. She could focus her employment efforts here."

"You're telling me that after a year of giving her the cold shoulder, you expect her to give up her life and move here to be with you after seeing you for one night?"

Huck took a big swig of his drink. He stared at the sunrays dancing on the water. A boat hummed by, creating waves, giving his vessel a good rocking. "If you knew our history, you'd think I was even more nuts. Thing is, no matter how hard I try, I can't get her out of my head. I've wanted to stay mad at her for lying to me. I told myself that's why I've stayed away, but that's just an excuse."

"If you're not upset with her for whatever lie she told you, then what's the problem?"

If he wanted to move forward with Aaliyah, he needed to be honest with himself and he might as well voice it to Cannon. He could either pack his bags and run, or he could dig his heels in and be fully engaged as a part of this team, like he'd told Knox at the party.

These men were his family. The family he chose. The people he wanted to be around.

And Aaliyah was the one. He knew that deep in his core. "I'm not good enough for her."

"That's a cop-out," Cannon said. "What are you really afraid of?"

"I have a past. It's not a pleasant one."

"We all have one of those. Does she know about this deep, dark secret?"

"She knows enough." He held up his finger. "But she only found out last night. She thought my brother was lying to her when he told her about the things that happened to us when we were kids and the things we had to do in order to survive."

"You have a brother?"

"Had. He died a year ago. She was his wife."

"Fuck, that's an interesting twist."

"He really didn't deserve a woman like her and if he were alive, I'd strangle him myself for what he did to her, but that's not the issue. While I know I'm not anything like my parents or my brother, I've had to cover up my past in order to have this amazing life. What if that catches up to me? What if your wife goes poking around someone who's tied to my life and finds the skeletons and decides to write a tell-all? What happens to her if I end up court-martialed?"

"Is it that bad?"

"You know Gunney Turnkey, right?" Huck polished off the rest of his sandwich and crumpled up his napkin and stuffed it back in his lunch bag. He checked his pole.

No action.

But again, it wasn't about catching anything. He couldn't care less if he got a single nibble.

"He's a legend. Did you know he went through bootcamp with Oz?"

"I heard that," Huck said. "Gunney saved my ass and he tried to help my brother, but he was a lost cause."

"Gunney was no saint," Cannon said. "He was a hired gun for the government. Black ops. And he did some sketchy shit in civilian life too."

"I'm well aware. But he had a code. And a good one. It worked for him and kept him out of trouble, even though he did some things that could have landed him in hot water. One of those things was what he did for me."

"If he handled it, then its buried so deep, no one is finding it," Cannon said. "And he wouldn't have done it if you hadn't been justified in your actions. I take it you were underage when this incident occurred."

"A few weeks shy of turning eighteen. Gunney assured me it was handled. That it could never touch me, but the real sucky thing was I hadn't done anything but defend myself. Had I not allowed my brother to cover up what happened in the first place, I wouldn't be in this position."

"Hey, man. It sounds like you're not in a bad place at all."

Huck leaned back and shifted his sunglasses on top of his head. "I don't trust my brother, even in death. Aaliyah had a recording of Sawyer telling her about the things I'd done. What if Sawyer told others? What if he has evidence somewhere?"

"It's been years since whatever you did was covered up. And what? A year since your brother died? If this was going to surface, I think it would have already. Gunney was a good man. If he thought you were going to run off the rails, he wouldn't have pushed you as hard as he did."

Huck laughed. Gunney suggested special forces training. It was Gunney that pushed Huck to be all that he could be and to put the past behind him. "What confuses me is that Gunney asked me to try to mend fences with my brother right before he died. He knew my brother hadn't changed his ways. That he was still a selfish asshole. So I don't understand why he sent me there."

"You said Aaliyah was your brother's wife, correct?"

Huck nodded.

"Did you ever think that maybe Gunney wasn't really asking you to get to know your brother, but to save his wife?"

Huck opened his mouth, but no words tumbled out. He hadn't thought about that, especially considering that at the end of Gunney's life, he'd been so sick it had been hard for him to communicate. He sometimes jumbled his sentences and words. The last time Huck had spoken to him, Gunney had begged him to go to Sawyer before it was too late.

To take care of it because he would regret it if he didn't.

Huck thought that meant fixing his relationship with Sawyer.

But now that he'd spoken to Cannon, perhaps Gunney meant something entirely different.

"Gunney told me that Sawyer and Aaliyah visited him when he was first diagnosed with cancer.

Maybe he saw something in Aaliyah, but he was too sick to do anything about it and the last few times I spoke to him, he could barely talk."

"I bet that's what he meant," Cannon said.

Huck had to agree. But it concerned him that someone out there still knew what he'd done. Not so much that he'd killed his mother in self-defense. But that he'd allowed it to be covered up and that someone else was serving time for the murder.

That man knew he hadn't killed Maribel Duncan. Why wasn't he talking?

"You don't look convinced. What's bothering you?" Cannon asked.

"A plethora of things." He set his feet on the fiberglass bottom and leaned forward. "Can I bare my soul?"

"Of course."

"There's a man named Charlie Crohns that's serving five life sentences for murder, one of which was my mother. Only, he didn't kill her, even though he confessed."

"Why would he do that?"

"That's a question I've never wanted to know the answer to until now."

"What does all this have to do with you telling Aaliyah that you love her?"

"I can't tell her how I really feel until I know without a shadow of a doubt that my past isn't going to come back and bite me in the ass and ruin her life. She's been through so much as it is. I'm willing to take responsibility for what happened. I always was. My brother took that choice from me and Gunney came in and cleaned it up as best he could, making sure I had a future. He always told me that if things had played out the right way, I could have had the same future I have right now."

"Do you believe that?"

"I do." Huck meant that. With his entire soul. He knew his mother would have beat him to a pulp. She was strung out on drugs and believed he had stolen from her, when it had been Sawyer. It had been pointless to argue with her and at first, he planned on taking his beating.

It was better that way.

But this was different. She came at him with a baseball bat and rage burning in her eyes. He'd never seen her that way before and from the very first fist to his face, he knew that she wasn't going to stop.

"But if it ever comes out that we covered up the truth, I'm fucked. My entire career in Delta Force is over. Everything I've worked so hard for is done."

"What if Jolene did some digging? She's

researched some interesting crimes and criminals over the years. She could find out why this inmate was so willing to take the fall."

"I don't know if that's a good idea and Aaliyah's going to leave in a couple of days. I worry that will poke a bear I can't afford to stir."

"Do you love Aaliyah and want to try to make a go of it with her?"

"I do," Huck finally admitted.

"Then I don't believe you have a choice." Cannon held up his cell. "Let's call Jolene and have her get the ball rolling, and then we should call Oz. He knew Gunney well. He'll know how to handle this so your career is unscathed no matter what happens and you have half a chance with Aaliyah. However, I have a suggestion for you."

"What's that?"

"We pull up lines and you haul ass back to Rocket's place and tell Aaliyah how you feel."

Huck's heart beat a little faster. He grabbed his pole and stared reeling it in. "What the fuck are you waiting for? I've got a woman I need to sweep off her feet."

"Care to explain what the heck happened at Huck's place earlier today? Or why you're packing?" Jayme asked, standing in the bedroom doorway with her hands on her hips and a scowl on her face.

Aaliyah let out a long sigh, tossed a shirt into her suitcase, and plopped onto the corner of the mattress. "I can't explain most of it, but in a nutshell, he can't forgive me for lying to him. It's too much of a betrayal because of things I can't tell you. Even though I think he's behaving like a spoiled child, I understand where he's coming from, and I would struggle with what I did if I were in his shoes."

"Do you really mean that?"

"Considering all that I learned, yes, I do. He's been hurt. It would be like me starting fresh with a man I didn't know. I'd be constantly worried his kindness would soon turn to a fist sandwich. Huck's protecting his heart, among other things."

"So, you're just going to pack up and leave? You're not going to fight for him after last night?"

"There's nothing here for me."

"I'm here." Jayme smiled. She sat next to Aaliyah and wrapped her arm around her shoulders. "You're giving up too fast."

"He knows I care about him, and I've told him everything. He even knows about the baby. There's nothing left for me to say or do. He doesn't want me. That's the truth."

"I don't believe that." Jayme ran her fingers through her hair like she used to do when they were kids. "What set him off this morning?"

"The baby. He hadn't read my medical records yet, so when he found out while having his morning coffee, he saw that as one last betrayal." Aaliyah left out the fact he'd had a wife who lied about a child before. That wasn't her story to tell. Besides, she didn't need him coming back that she'd broken his trust.

Again.

"He just needs time to process," Jayme said.

"Perhaps, however, I need off this roller-coaster

ride I've put myself on. I need to get my life back on track. I've got interviews set up in a couple of weeks. I need to focus on getting a new career off the ground, and all this has been a distraction," Aaliyah said. "My flight leaves in three hours. Can you take me to the airport, or should I call an Uber?"

"I can take you, but I wish you wouldn't go. Rocket and the kids won't be back in time to say goodbye."

"I'm sorry, Jayme, but I can't stay a second longer. I made a mistake in coming in the first place. Huck has too much baggage. He's carrying so much from his past and he'll never be able to let it go. It's impossible."

"Why do you say that?"

"While he's nothing like Sawyer and he doesn't have a mean bone in his body, he's haunted by the same things."

"I'm not following," Jayme said, palming her cheek. "And don't you dare start making excuses for Sawyer. He beat you both physically and emotionally. He held you prisoner. He manipulated you and made you dependent on him financially so you were trapped and couldn't leave. He was a horrible human being."

"I know that. I'm the one who lived it. But

Sawyer and Huck were raised by the same people. They lived the same life. As boys, they were forced to make similar choices. Sawyer did have a moral compass. Just not when it came to women. He had no respect for us. He believed we were second-class citizens and should obey our husbands. He got that from the fact his mother never listened to their father. The stories he told me about how his parents would fight were horrifying."

"His dad beat his mom too?"

"Yes and no," Aaliyah said. "They fought." She lifted her hands, made fists, and punched the air. "But it was his mother who won, every single time. It demasculinized Sawyer. He saw his father as being weak, a less than man for taking any kind of flak from a woman."

"She was just standing up for herself. So, I say good for her." Jayme nodded.

"No. Their mother was a piece of shit. She would often start the fights. It was their dad who was the one defending himself."

"Oh. I see." Jayme slumped. "That's a fucked-up childhood."

"There's a lot I can't tell you because it's not my story to tell and I wouldn't do that to Huck. He's a very private man. I've already outed him enough with the men he works with and he's not happy about that."

Jayme tilted her head and smiled. "These men are his family. Sometimes more so than the ones they come from, or the ones they create with their wives and children. They have to know who exactly they are working with inside and out because they are called upon to protect and serve not just our country, but each other. I've heard rumblings from Cannon and the others on Huck's team that they need him to open up more. I'm not saying you should do it for him, you shouldn't, but everyone here has a past."

"Huck's is complicated. He's a good man. The best. He has the kindest soul of any person I've ever met. Only he can't see it. All he sees is the past. The one thing that he did and because of his brother's actions, Huck feels trapped and he's trying to shield me from it, which is sweet on the one hand, but so not necessary. All our secrets are out in the open. At least between us they are. They can't hurt us."

"Yes, they can." Huck's deep voice bounced off the walls and vibrated in her ears.

She jumped, nearly falling off the edge of the bed. "Shit. You scared me." She stood, smoothing down the front of her jeans.

"Sorry." He stepped into the room and leaned against the dresser.

"I'll leave the two of you alone." Jayme smiled before practically running out and down the hall.

Huck closed the bedroom door. "I didn't mean to eavesdrop."

"How much of that conversation did you hear?"

"Just the last few sentences and you're right. I could only see how my brother forced me to cover up something that wasn't a crime, but he made it one," Huck said. "I've been living in fear my entire life that it will come back to destroy the life I created. That's what Sawyer was going to do to me when he found out about us."

"What do you mean?" she whispered.

"The more I thought about it the more I realized that he needed you to panic. He wanted you to fight back more than you'd ever done before. He needed to come up with a narrative of his own. One that when the police came and you were dead and neither him nor I were, he could spin it so that he came out smelling like a rose and I was the bad guy."

Her heart dropped like a brick to the pit of her stomach. She opened her mouth but the only thing that came out was a noise that sounded like a dying cow.

"He wanted to ruin me and as long as Gunney was alive, he couldn't. Gunney made sure of that."

"Why not?"

"Gunney knew everything. Right down to the truth about how Sawyer killed my dad. Could he prove it? Not beyond a shadow of a doubt, but he knew enough to cast reasonable suspicion. Of course, so do I, but I couldn't say shit because of what my brother had on me. It was always tit for tat between me and Sawyer." Huck inched closer. "Sawyer's plan was never to kill me; it was to make sure my career was ruined and I went to prison. You were collateral damage. I'm sorry I didn't see it sooner."

"It doesn't change the outcome of what happened. He was still going to kill me."

Huck reached out and ran his thumb across her cheek. "Yes. He was and that's what I can't forgive myself for. Every time I look at you, I see your eyes beaten closed. The bruises on your face." He leaned in and kissed her forehead. "The broken ribs and arm. The scars he's left on your body. I allowed that to happen."

She opened her mouth, but he shushed her with a tender kiss. "I know I can't go back and change what happened. I understand you don't blame me for what he did to you that night or what you had to do in order to defend yourself. However, you're going to have to give me time to learn to live with the consequences of my inaction."

Resting her hands on his strong frame, she stared into his intense gaze.

He looked past her and frowned. "Are you packing?"

"I was going to leave tonight."

"Don't go." He took her chin with his thumb and forefinger. "I can't promise you anything other than my willingness to try. I want to see where things might go."

"That's enough for me." She expected him to smile and plant a wet kiss on her mouth, but he didn't. Instead, he took a step back. "What's wrong?"

"I've asked Cannon's fiancée to look into the man who took the fall for my mother's murder."

"Why? Why would you do that?" she screeched. Her muscles trembled. It made no sense that he'd stir up trouble for himself that way.

"Oz knew Gunney pretty well and knows other people like me that Gunney helped. Oz is going to do some checking into what the likelihood is that my past can reach forward into my present and future."

"Huck. I don't understand why this matters."

"Because Sawyer had three days to plan my demise. You have to remember he used our mother's death as a way to control me. To make sure I'd always did what he wanted."

"Sawyer was a control freak, that's for sure," she said. "How did Gunney even come into your lives?"

"He went to high school with our dad. Grew up in the same town. He'd come back every once in a while. Local hero kind of thing. But there were always rumors about him being a hired hitman for the government."

"That's what Sawyer said about you. He always told me you were a dangerous man and that you worked outside the law. That's why he didn't have a relationship with you."

"Well, that's not why we never had a relationship, but I am Delta Force and that's a fancy way of saying I have done some things for the government in the name of freedom that the average American doesn't ever need to know about, much less want to hear."

"I've heard a few things through Jayme and that was enough," she admitted. "Why didn't Gunney force Sawyer into the military?"

"Oh. There was no forcing me into it. I wanted it hook, line, and sinker. College was not for me. I sucked at school. Hated it. Sawyer thrived in that environment and he wouldn't have lasted five minutes in bootcamp. Me? Holy shit, it was like coming home. Gunney had a way of reading people. He knew what we needed and he made sure we got it. Sawyer would have ended up working for some mobster, so honestly, Gunney saved him in many ways. But no one could take away his anger toward our mother."

"But you didn't carry that with you." She raised up on tiptoe and kissed his cheek. "You respect women."

"Trust me. I have mommy anger issues out my ass. But hitting anyone isn't the way to solve problems. Abuse is about control and power. Sawyer and I never had any and he spent his adult life trying to obtain it through becoming rich and by exerting what he thought was power over women."

"And you?"

Huck shrugged. "I have no thirst for power and I learned a long time ago and it was proven to me with my ex-wife that the only thing I control is myself."

"Then why are you going to go looking for trouble by poking the past?"

"My ex-wife used to tell me all the time that she

thought I was distant. Cold even. That I was constantly looking over my shoulder. And she'd be right. I was always worried my dirty little secret was going to come crashing down and ruin our lives. It's probably what pushed her into the arms of another man."

"That was her doing, not yours."

"True, but our marriage was struggling and I wasn't helping," he said. "The point is that in order for you and me to have any real chance of a future together, I need to know that there is no way I could wind up being court-martialed and in prison."

"Could it really come to that?"

"Based on what Gunney told me when I enlisted, no. But I have no idea what my brother might have set in motion. He doesn't play by the same rules, and he made that clear when he didn't go to the police the night my mother died."

"So what's the plan then?"

"We start with me getting on an airplane tomorrow morning with Jolene and seeing if Charlie Chrons, the man who went to prison for killing my mother, will have a chat with us."

"Is that really necessary?"

"If anyone out there knows what really happened, I need to be prepared for the worst."

"Then I'm coming with you."

"No."

Before she could respond, he kissed her. Hard. With intent. It was wild. Passionate. She wrapped her arms around his thick body. She didn't want to let go.

The sound of someone clearing their throat caught her attention.

She dropped her head to his chest.

"Sorry to interrupt," Rocket said. "Jayme wants to know if the two of you are staying for dinner."

"I could eat. Are you hungry?" Huck cupped her cheeks.

"Famished," she said.

"We'll be right there." He held her gaze for a long moment. "I care about you. A lot. Because of that, I won't risk putting you in a bad place. Can you understand that?"

"More than you know."

CHAPTER 9

"Did he give us a reason why he won't see you?" Huck paced in his backyard. He'd barely been able to sleep last night. Even having Aaliyah at his side hadn't helped his restlessness.

In some ways it made it worse.

All he wanted was to be able to actually leave the past where it belonged. He resented the fuck out of his brother for putting him in this position to begin with. Had they simply called the police when their mother died, none of this would be happening now.

He appreciated everything that Jolene and Cannon were doing for him, but he still felt helpless. It was a familiar feeling from his childhood and he hated it. Once he joined the Army, he believed he had some control over his destiny, but there was always this dark cloud hanging over his head, and he wished it would either downpour or go away. One or the other because it following him around had gotten real old.

He glanced at his watch. If they were going to catch this flight, they needed to leave in the next hour.

"He doesn't want to be in any book," Jolene said. "I explained that I wasn't even sure I was going to do a book on any of these murders and this was strictly an interview. He told me to fuck off."

"Nice," Huck said with a sarcastic tone. "What if we told him that I wanted to talk?"

"I don't know." Jolene let out a long breath. "I didn't like the idea of you coming with me. The last thing you need is him going back on his word. Even the hint of you doing something wrong could bring an investigation. We don't want that."

"I agree," Cannon said.

"Fuck. I wish I could just let this go, but I can't."

"I hear you," Jolene said. "I wish I knew what Oz wanted and why we can't leave for the airport until he gets here."

"I don't know. He said it was important and he had to talk to you in person," Cannon said.

Aaliyah opened the sliding glass doors. "Breakfast is served." She lifted a tray and stepped outside.

"That smells fabulous," Jolene said.

Huck took the tray and helped Aaliyah set the table.

She'd outdone herself with homemade crepes and strawberry filling.

It felt almost normal to have another couple over with him and Aaliyah to break bread. Like this was something they did on a regular basis.

It was certainly something he wanted to do again.

"Oh, my God. This is delicious." Jolene raised her fork. "You're going to have to give me the recipe."

"It's ridiculously easy." Aaliyah made herself another plate and loaded it with whip cream. "Are you still going to go even though Charlie made it clear he won't see you?"

"I think it's a waste of time," Cannon said. "Besides, whatever Oz has to say, he told me not to let the two of you leave for the airport before he gets here."

"I'm beginning to think Gunney knew everyone." Huck knew Gunney's reach was far and wide. He'd been around the block and worked on a lot of missions with a lot of different teams. Gunney was the kind of guy that people thought was a loner, but he wasn't. If there was ever a time to remember the old cliche not to judge a book by its cover, Gunney was it.

"Gunney worked with Oz's team back in the day on some black ops mission. I don't know the details," Cannon said. "But it was back when my brother Tony was in Delta Force."

"Did Tony know Gunney?" Huck asked.

"He did," Cannon confirmed. "Not as well as Oz, but they were all on the same mission together. They saw some serious shit on that mission."

"I can only imagine." Huck tossed his napkin on his plate and leaned back. He reached under the table and took Aaliyah's hand. "Gunney told me some stories after I signed on the dotted line that made me question what I'd gotten myself into."

"Tony refused to tell me shit in fear I'd backpedal." Cannon laughed. "Though he did tell me that if I was looking for normal, the military wasn't it. Turns out, he was the one who needed conventional and it looked good on Tony."

"He's a great teacher," Jolene said. "So's his wife."

"I'm sorry I didn't get a chance to meet them at the party." Aaliyah ran her thumb over the back of his hand.

He desperately wanted to know that this was his

chance at a new beginning. That he and Aaliyah would get their opportunity to get to know one another the way normal people did.

Well, maybe not exactly that way since his feelings for her were so strong there was no turning back.

"There'll be plenty of time for that." Jolene stood. "Cannon, why don't you help me with these dishes."

"You don't have to do that," Aaliyah said.

"We insist." Jolene smiled. "Don't we, honey?"

"That we do." Cannon followed his fiancée into the house, carrying a tray full of plates.

"They're a nice couple." Aaliyah tucked her hair behind her ears. "I just finished one of her books. She's incredibly talented."

"I'll have to take your word for it," Huck said. "I've never been much of a book reader. But everyone raves about her work. Especially Lefty and his wife Kinley."

"Ah. *The Alleyway Strangler*," Aaliyah said. "I've heard that was an amazing book; I just haven't read it."

"You should. Jolene is the real deal."

Huck leaned closer and pressed his lips over Aaliyah's mouth. She tasted like strawberries and sugar. Everything about her was beyond perfect.

"I'm sorry you had to go through the miscarriage alone."

She gasped.

"I should have read your letters."

"It's okay," she said.

"Nothing about what you've been through is okay. I'm going to find ways to make it up to you."

She smiled and it melted his heart.

"Hey, Huck," Cannon called. "Oz is here."

"We'll be right in." He stood, lifting her into his arms. "Let's go hear what he's found out, and then I'm getting on that plane and I'm going to find a way to have a chat with this Charlie guy."

Huck sat on the sofa with Aaliyah snuggled next to him. He wasn't having this conversation without her even though Oz had originally thought it might be best.

"What have you found out?" Huck asked as he squeezed Aaliyah's thigh.

"It's not what I've found; it's what I know." Oz leaned forward in his chair and rested his hands on his knees.

Huck didn't know Oz all that well. He'd done

training with Oz's team when he'd first joined his and the two teams often worked in tandem. However, Huck had done his best to do his job and keep to himself as much as possible, especially when it came to those men with families. It wasn't that he didn't want to get to know the people he worked with, he did. It was imperative that they understood each other, but Huck had yet to find a team to call his home. The closest he'd come to that had been when he'd been married, but that ended when his marriage came to a halt and he begged for a transfer. Since then, Huck had been the odd man out.

This current team made it difficult for him to keep his distance. Or maybe it wasn't them. Perhaps it was him.

"I worked with Gunney on a mission years ago. When all was said and done, he asked me to do him a favor," Oz said. "I kind of owed him since he saved my life, so I said yes." Oz took an envelope that he'd set on the floor and tossed it at Huck. "Gunney didn't think I'd ever need this, but he asked me to hold on to it for safekeeping."

"He did that all those years ago?"

"No," Oz said. "This was about ten years ago. Then when he was diagnosed with cancer, he came to me again and asked if I could find a way for you to be transferred here. There wasn't an opening until after he died. Well, until after your brother died, but I pulled some strings and made sure it happened."

"You've got to be kidding me." Huck gripped the envelope and nearly tore it apart. "My being here was orchestrated?"

"Yes. But you're a good fit. Everyone thinks so. If I could have found a way to bring you over sooner, I would have. Obviously, he had no clue about you and Aaliyah."

"Obviously," Huck muttered. "What's in this?" Sometimes it was better to get the abridged version than to have to read through it himself.

"A lot of people owed Gunney favors," Oz said. "That's how Oz got someone to agree to take on one more murder rap."

"Charlie Chrons," Huck said.

Oz nodded. "That was his name. Gunney set up the trial and made sure someone was put behind bars on appearances and he has an insurance policy if Sawyer ever decided to change his story."

"What might that be?" It amazed Huck how Gunney thought of every detail.

"Forensic evidence that proves your brother murdered your dad. That he's the one who covered up what really happened to your mom. That Sawyer acted alone and that you had no idea what he was doing until it was too late." Oz pointed to the envelope. "That's what's in there. Along with the proof that you acted in self-defense the night your mother died."

Huck's heart beat so hard and loud it was all he could focus on. He glanced between the papers in his hands and Oz. "You knew this about me all along?"

Oz nodded.

"You pushed to bring me to this team when Skip was injured."

"I tried to bring you here before that, but I'm glad it was this team. It's a better fit. Not that I wished anyone be hurt. Skip's a good man and he was a member of this family. But so are you." Oz sat up a little taller. "My wife and I, we take on foster kids from time to time. Gunney knew that I'd have a soft spot for your story. The only thing you did wrong was being a dumbass scared young boy who had been living in a man's world since the day he was born."

"I appreciate that," Huck said. "But what if this Charlie guy talks?"

"For the record, there's no Charlie and that's why he's refusing to see you." Oz reached for the coffee mug on the end table and brought it to his lips.

"That makes no sense. They arrested him. He plead guilty and went to prison. We called." Huck narrowed his stare. His chest tightened. He didn't like unanswered questions. Especially when they led to more.

"Gunney knew people in high places who could do things. One of them would be to create a narrative to make sure you never got into trouble for something Sawyer did."

Huck stood. He rubbed the back of his neck. "But it was Sawyer who did all the grunt work in framing this Charlie guy before Gunney came into the picture." Or did he? Huck froze as he forced his mind to go back in time and search the archives of his memory. While he thought constantly about the consequences of that day and what happened in the week following, he never, not once, allowed himself to replay the events.

It was too painful.

He closed his eyes.

Quick flashes of his mother in a full-out rage, verbally accosting him and his brother. But Sawyer was egging Huck on, telling him to fight back while his mother was calling him names, telling him he was weak and didn't have the balls to stand up to anyone.

It was as if Sawyer wanted him to do it.

Then Sawyer handed his mother the baseball bat and Huck a knife.

What the fuck? Why would Sawyer do that?

"Huck. Are you okay?" Aaliyah's voice tickled his mind, bringing him partially into the present, but not completely.

He needed to play this tape. To remember everything. "Yes. I need a moment to think." He blinked, catching her gaze.

She curled her fingers around his biceps and squeezed.

"I'm fine. Really. I need a little fresh air while I recall exactly what happened. It's been a while since I've allowed myself to play it all the way through."

"Take all the time you need," Oz said.

"Do you want me to come with you?" Aaliyah asked.

"Sure." His answer surprised himself. He took her by the hand and led her outside.

"What's going on? You look as though you're in pain."

"I kind of am," he admitted as he leaned against the fence. "I'm remembering the night my mother died and it's not what I've been telling myself. Well, not exactly."

"What do you mean?"

"I don't even remember what set her off. I think it was something about eating the last of the leftover pizza. Which was Sawyer, not me, but it never mattered. She was yelling at me about being a shit son. Pointing her finger in my face and forcing me to back up. Sawyer was telling me to fight back for a change. To be a man. And then, and this I didn't remember until just now, Sawyer handed my mother that baseball bat and me a knife. Up until that point, she only used her fists. I couldn't hit a woman. Especially my mother. It wasn't in my nature. It had nothing to do with how I was raised because trust me, I wasn't raised to be anything but a criminal."

Aaliyah leaned into him and wrapped her arms around his shoulders. "That goes to show you what a good person you are."

"I don't know about that."

She tilted her head and glared.

He kissed her nose. He didn't deserve to have someone so wonderful in his life. "I don't know why I didn't recall Sawyer giving my mom that bat and me a knife, but it changed the dynamic of the fight. She cracked a couple ribs that day. Broke my wrist and gave me one hell of a concussion. That was before I was able to get it out of her hands and return the favor. Only, I used the knife. She fell and landed on a glass table. That was it." He blew out a puff of air. "I sat on the floor next to her for three hours. I didn't move. I didn't cry. I didn't say a word. My brother left. I had no idea what he was doing. I figured calling the police or something. When he came back, he had people with him and they started staging things. He had me go clean up and leave. Next thing I knew, I was being told a story about how I was at a friend's house and I was never to say anything otherwise. A day later, Gunney showed up and told me to stick to that and he'd take care of everything. For both of us."

"Sounds like Oz knows exactly what Gunney did." She palmed his cheek. "Why don't we go back inside and find out?"

Huck nodded. He wanted a future. With Aaliyah. This was how he got it.

He made his way back into the family room. He felt as though all eyes were on him as he sat down on the sofa. "Tell me how there's no Charlie."

"Gunney was at the local watering hole when he overheard Sawyer looking for some asshole who knew a guy in the cleaning business. If you get my drift," Oz said with an amused smile. "He couldn't believe Sawyer would even use that language. Or be so public about it. So Gunney got involved in true Gunney style. The story that Sawyer told Gunney couldn't have happened."

Heat burned across Huck's skin. "Did he tell Gunney I did it in cold blood?"

"Something like that. But Gunney's no fool. The team that came in your mom's house that day were professionals. Retired black ops for hire. Granted, they do some shady shit as long as they get paid."

Huck's heart exploded with rage. And hatred. It was like pouring gas on a fire. "Why didn't Gunney tell me this?"

"He never wanted you to know unless it was necessary," Oz said.

"Why did he want me to go mend fences? Because that's what he said right before he died." Huck tried not to allow the anger and resentment to fill his soul, but it crept in like a slow leak from a faucet. "I thought maybe it was some kind of cryptic message to help Aaliyah."

"It may have been," Oz said. "Or it could have been that the cancer and the treatment had done such a number on him that he didn't really know what he was saying. Or maybe a combination of both."

Huck knew that statement could very well be

true. The last couple of times he spoke with Gunney, he didn't always make sense. He'd mix things up. Not only would he mess up times and dates, but people too.

"Gunney thought of you as family. He wanted to do right by you. His team had gathered enough evidence to prove it was self-defense. But instead, they set the scene to be murder. They put a ghost in to take the fall and pulled him as soon as the press died down, which was pretty damn quick. It's a rare occasion that anyone ever comes looking for Charlie Chrons. Whenever someone does, our ghost makes an appearance. But not really and he doesn't take visitors."

"I can imagine that might be hard since he doesn't exist," Huck mumbled. "I can't believe Gunney did all that."

"He wished he'd done more."

"What does that mean? What did Gunney find out?"

"Two years ago, Gunny heard from someone who got a case of the guilts that Sawyer's plan wasn't going to frame someone else; he was going to make it look like you hid the body and then lead the cops to it so he could look like a damn hero."

"Are you fucking kidding me?" Huck said. He

squeezed Aaliyah's hand. Tight. Perhaps too tight since she wiggled her fingers. "Who told him that?"

"It doesn't matter anymore. The source passed away and he'd been the only other person that knew Sawyer's plan from start to finish."

"Leroy," Huck said softly. "He'd been Sawyer's best friend for years. But after my brother went to college, they stopped hanging together."

"Probably had more to do with what happened that night than anything else."

"I would think so," Huck said with a long sigh. "I remember Gunney asking me questions about Sawyer. It was like he was trying to get me to give him a reason to send him up the river. I couldn't do it. Even though I knew Sawyer would turn on me in a heartbeat. I figured if I got out of town, joined the Army, that would be it. We could be brothers who never saw each other and barely talked, which is what we became. I gave Gunney the green light to help Sawyer."

"You're a good man," Oz said. "You got a second chance; why shouldn't your brother get one. You can't second-guess these decisions. Gunney didn't."

He wrapped his arm around Aaliyah. Sawyer's second chance caused her a world of hurt. Something he felt personally responsible for, and yet he couldn't help but wonder if they'd be sitting on this couch if he turned back the hands of time and changed one tiny little detail of either of their pasts.

That was a mindfuck if he ever put himself through one.

"I appreciate you telling me all this," Huck said. "Can I ask you something?"

"Of course." Oz nodded.

"Would you have told me if Aaliyah had not come looking for me?"

"Probably not," Oz said. "Gunney thought you were living your best life. Other than your divorce, he didn't see a reason to rock the boat."

That made sense. Until Aaliyah, Huck dealt with history by keeping it at bay. It worked just fine because there was no part of that life that had fingers in his present.

"Thanks for being honest," Huck said.

"Anytime." Oz stood. "I need to get home. I've got a houseful of kids that need my attention. If you have any questions or just want to talk, don't ever hesitate."

"I'll be right back." Huck kissed Aaliyah. "Why don't you go find Cannon and Jolene?"

"It was nice to meet you, Oz." Aaliyah stretched out her hand.

"Likewise," Oz said.

Huck walked Oz to the front door. "One last thing. Does anyone else know all this?"

"On my team? Yeah. Everyone," Oz admitted. "No one knew on your team."

"Then how'd Gunney get me here?"

Oz laughed and slapped Huck on the back. "I learned over the years never to question how that man got anything done. Now I'm in his position and all I'll tell you is that not only are you here because Gunney made it happen, but you're here because I want you here. And you belong here. Now, you and that pretty young lady out there have some dating to do. I suggest you do it."

Huck smiled. "Yes, sir."

"Don't fucking call me that again."

Huck stood in the doorway. He stared out into the hot Texas morning sun. In all the places he'd lived, this was the first one that felt like home.

"Hey," Aaliyah whispered as she wrapped her arm around his waist. "Cannon and Jolene are in the kitchen making more coffee. They invited us to their place for a barbecue. They might invite a couple other people. Are you up for it?"

"Are you asking me on a date?" He turned and pulled her tight to his chest.

She tilted her head. "Why, yes. I am."

"I'd love to." His past was finally where it belonged and he could live without worrying if it was going to catch up to his future.

This was his time and he planned on enjoying it.

With Aaliyah.

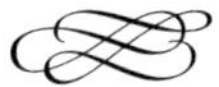

CHAPTER 10

Two months later...

Aaliyah raced through the airport, gripping the most important letter of her life. She couldn't believe it. Everything was falling into place. Life couldn't have been more perfect.

Well, except maybe if she could find a job in Texas so she could quit the temporary one she had in Upstate, New York.

Her cell vibrated in her hand as she stepped outside. The hot, humid Texas air filled her lungs.

Home.

At least she wanted to call it home again.

Maybe it was too soon.

She and Huck had only been together for two months. In that time frame, she'd been flying back and forth as often as she could. However, he'd been called away on a mission ten days ago and he'd been gone ever since. Yesterday, she received word he'd be back today. All she wanted to do was surprise him by being at his place when he returned.

Fucking flight delays might have ruined that one.

She lifted her phone.

Jolene: *Running late. Traffic is horrible. Be there in ten. Tops.*

Shit. Just what she needed. She tapped the screen. He should be on the base, but he wouldn't be able to reach out until after he'd been debriefed. She understood that. However, he could be getting in his truck and heading home when he did that and he lived closer to the base than the airport.

Aaliyah: *Have you heard anything?*

Jolene: *No.*

If the boys were able to communicate yet, Jolene would have heard from Cannon. They were getting married in three weeks. Jolene wasn't generally the nervous type, but she had become a bit of a jittery bride.

Aaliyah couldn't blame her. It was a lot of planning for one day.

If she ever had the opportunity to do it again, she would have a small ceremony. Just a few close personal friends. Nothing fancy. No big white dress.

She really needed to stop thinking about all that stuff. She was just caught up in Jolene's moment. She and Huck were fine right where they were. Besides, she hadn't even moved to Texas yet.

She smiled. He was going to be so happy when she told him the news.

Finding an empty bench, she sat down and set her backpack between her legs. She quickly texted Jolene where she had perched herself so it would be easy for Jolene to find her. She took the letter and scanned it one last time.

A job working at as a data analyst for a large marketing company out of Dallas that had an office right in Killeen. She could start next week.

Honk.

Honk. Honk.

Honk.

Honk. Honk. Honk.

Stuffing the paper in her purse, she glanced up. A policeman had stopped traffic, only allowing one line of cars to pass.

What the hell?

She leaned forward so she could get a better look.

She couldn't decide if it looked like a funeral or a parade, Texas style, since they were all big old pickups.

There were signs on the sides of the vehicles.

First one read: *WILL.*

Next one: *YOU.*

The third truck had a big sash with the word: *MARRY.*

"Aw. That's a cute way to propose," a woman standing near her said.

She stood, glancing in both directions, looking for a man on bended knee, but found no one.

More honking caught her attention.

A black SUV stopped in front of her.

It had a sign that read: *ME, AALIYAH?*

She gasped. Her heart jumped to the back of her throat, pounding out of control before dropping to her gut.

Those signs couldn't be for her, could they?

She blinked, trying to focus on her surroundings. The rear passenger door opened and Huck appeared wearing his fatigues.

And a big old Texas smile.

His entire team got out of the vehicles. As did Oz and his team. Along with all the wives and children.

Including Jolene who gave her a little wink and a wave.

"Hey," Huck said casually as if he hadn't created quite the fanfare.

"What are you doing?" she whispered.

"Isn't that obvious?" He turned and waved his hand toward the caravan of pickups. "Oh. I guess I should do this proper." He dug into his pocket and pulled out a sparkling diamond ring. Keeping his gaze locked with hers, he got on bended knee. "I've loved you since we first met and while we had a rough start, I was hoping you'd give me the honor of loving you every day for the rest of our days. What do you say? Aaliyah, will you marry me?" He slipped the ring on her finger. It fit perfectly.

"Now I know why you were being so weird with the measuring tape."

"That's not an answer."

She giggled. "Yes. Of course I'll marry you."

He jumped to both feet and lifted her in the air, twirling her around.

There were cheers and clapping and whistles in the background.

"That was quite the proposal," she whispered in his ear.

"I don't want to go another day without us being

together forever." He took her chin with his thumb and forefinger. "I know you like being independent. One of the things I love about you, but can you just quit your job and move here?"

"I already quit."

He jerked his head back.

She laughed. "I got a new one and I start next week." She kissed her fiancé with purpose. She didn't care that all their friends and family were looking on or that perfect strangers were passing by.

This was what life had in store for her and she had no regrets. Not anymore.

She was exactly where she belonged.

One year later...

Huck raced through the hospital. He smelled like thirty hours on the back of a transport plane.

It was six weeks too soon.

It wasn't supposed to happen like this.

This was his last deployment, and then he'd be home until the baby was born.

He skidded to a stop at the information desk at the labor and delivery floor. "I'm... I'm... I'm..."

"Just breathe, sir," a young man in a nurse's uniform said. "Are you Captain Duncan?"

"I am."

"Come with me."

Huck took in a deep breath and let it out slowly, willing his heart rate to come down to normal levels. "Where are you taking me?"

"To your wife, Aaliyah Duncan."

"Is she okay?"

"She's doing great," the young man said. "I'm George. I'm her nurse."

"Oh. Okay. What about the baby? All I know is that she went into labor three days ago and they were going to try to stop it or slow it down. I've been in transport ever since."

George stopped in front of a door. "Your wife is in this room." He squeezed Huck's shoulder. "I'll let her fill you in on everything."

Huck wasn't sure if that was a good thing or not. But he wasn't going to wait another second. He nodded to the nurse and barreled into the room.

He stopped dead in his tracks and gawked at his wife, nursing a baby.

His baby.

Their baby.

"You made it," Aaliyah said as she rubbed the top of the tiny child's head. "Come here."

He swallowed. "Not in time." He sat on the edge of the bed, in total awe. "Are you okay?"

"Yes." She smiled. "This is our son."

"A boy?"

She nodded with tears in her eyes. "He looks so small, but the doctors say he's big for when he was born and he doesn't seem to have any problems."

Tears burned the corners of his eyes. He leaned over and kissed his son's forehead and then pressed his lips to his wife's. "What did you name him?"

"I was waiting for you since you were so sure it was girl and only agreed on a girl's name."

He chuckled.

"What about Gunner?" he said softly.

"I think that's a fine name."

Huck eased onto the bed and looped his arm around mother and child. He never knew his life could be so full of joy and happiness.

Thank you for reading Shielding Aaliyah. Please feel free to leave an HONEST review!

Sign up for my Newsletter (https://dl.bookfunnel. com/82gm8b9k4y) where I often give away free books before publication.

. . .

Join my private Facebook group (https://www.facebook. com/groups/191706547909047/) where I post exclusive excerpts and discuss all things murder and love!

Never miss a new release. Follow me on Amazon:amazon.com/author/jentalty

And on Bookbub: bookbub.com/authors/jen-talty

<u>**FLY WITH ME**</u>

Club Temptation
<u>**SWEET TEMPTATION**</u>

The Monroes
<u>**COLOR ME YOURS**</u>

<u>**COLOR ME SMART**</u>

<u>**COLOR ME FREE**</u>

<u>**COLOR ME LUCKY**</u>

<u>**COLOR ME ICE**</u>

It's all in the Whiskey
<u>**JOHNNIE WALKER**</u>

<u>**GEORGIA MOON**</u>

<u>**JACK DANIELS**</u>

<u>**JIM BEAM**</u>

<u>**WHISKEY SOUR**</u>

<u>**WHISKEY COBBLER**</u>

<u>**WHISKEY SMASH**</u>

Search and Rescue
<u>**PROTECTING AINSLEY**</u>

<u>**PROTECTING CLOVER**</u>

<u>**PROTECTING OLYMPIA**</u>

<u>**PROTECTING FREEDOM**</u>

<u>**PROTECTING PRINCESS**</u>

NY STATE TROOPER SERIES

<u>*In Two Weeks*</u>

<u>*Dark Water*</u>

<u>*Deadly Secrets*</u>

<u>*Murder in paradise Bay*</u>

<u>*To Protect His own*</u>

<u>*Deadly Seduction*</u>

<u>*When A Stranger Calls*</u>

<u>*His Deadly Past*</u>

<u>*The Corkscrew Killer*</u>

Brand New Novella for the First Responders series

A spin off from the NY State Troopers series

<u>**PLAYING WITH FIRE**</u>

<u>**PRIVATE CONVERSATION**</u>

<u>**THE RIGHT GROOM**</u>

<u>**AFTER THE FIRE**</u>

<u>**CAUGHT IN THE FLAMES**</u>

The Men of Thief Lake

REKINDLED

DESTINY'S DREAM

Federal Investigators

JANE DOE'S RETURN

THE BUTTERFLY MURDERS

The Aegis Network

THE LIGHTHOUSE

HER LAST HOPE

THE LAST FLIGHT

THE RETURN HOME

THE MATRIARCH

The Collective Order

THE LOST SISTER

THE LOST SOLDIER

THE LOST SOUL

THE LOST CONNECTION

A Spin-Off Series: Witches Academy Series

THE NEW ORDER

Special Forces Operation Alpha

BURNING DESIRE

BURNING KISS

BURNING SKIES

BURNING LIES

BURNING HEART

BURNING BED

REMEMBER ME ALWAYS

The Brotherhood Protectors

Out of the Wild

ROUGH JUSTICE

ROUGH AROUND THE EDGES

ROUGH RIDE

ROUGH EDGE

ROUGH BEAUTY

The Brotherhood Protectors

The Saving Series

SAVING LOVE

SAVING MAGNOLIA

SAVING LEATHER

Hot Hunks

Cove's Blind Date Blows Up

My Everyday Hero – Ledger

Tempting Tavor

Holiday Romances

A CHRISTMAS GETAWAY

ALASKAN CHRISTMAS

WHISPERS

CHRISTMAS IN THE SAND

CHRISTMAS IN JULY

Heroes & Heroines on the Field

TAKING A RISK

TEE TIME

A New Dawn

THE BLIND DATE

SPRING FLING

SUMMERS GONE

WINTER WEDDING

Witches and Werewolves

LADY SASS

ALL THAT SASS

ABOUT THE AUTHOR

Jen Talty is the *USA Today* Bestselling Author of Contemporary Romance, Romantic Suspense, and Paranormal Romance. In the fall of 2020, her short story was selected and featured in a 1001 Dark Nights Anthology. She is currently contracted to write a new series with Kristen Proby's Lady Boss Press, as well as Susan Stoker's *Special Forces: Operation Alpha* and Elle James's *Brotherhood Protectors.*

Regardless of the genre, her goal is to take you on a ride that will leave you floating under the sun with warmth in your heart. She writes stories about broken heroes and heroines who aren't necessarily looking for romance, but in the end, they find the kind of love books are written about :).

She first started writing while carting her kids to one hockey rink after the other, averaging 170 games per year between 3 kids in 2 countries and 5 states. Her first book, IN TWO WEEKS was originally published in 2007. In 2010 she helped form a publishing company (Cool Gus Publishing) with *NY Times* Bestselling Author Bob Mayer where she ran the technical side of the business through 2016.

Jen is currently enjoying the next phase of her life… the empty nester! She and her husband reside in Jupiter, Florida.

Grab a glass of vino, kick back, relax, and let the romance roll in…

Sign up for my Newsletter (https://dl.bookfunnel. com/82gm8b9k4y) where I often give away free books before publication.

Join my private Facebook group (https://www.facebook. com/groups/191706547909047/) where I post exclusive excerpts and discuss all things murder and love!

Never miss a new release. Follow me on Amazon:amazon.com/author/jentalty

And on Bookbub: bookbub.com/authors/jen-talty

Jordan Dane: Redemption for Avery
Tarina Deaton: Found in the Lost
Aspen Drake, Intense
KL Donn: Unraveling Love
Riley Edwards: Protecting Olivia
PJ Fiala: Defending Sophie
Nicole Flockton: Protecting Maria
Hope Ford: Rescuing Karina
Alexa Gregory: Backdraft
Michele Gwynn: Rescuing Emma
Casey Hagen: Shielding Nebraska
Desiree Holt: Protecting Maddie
Kathy Ivan: Saving Sarah
Kris Jacen, Be With Me
Jesse Jacobson: Protecting Honor
Silver James: Rescue Moon
Becca Jameson: Saving Sofia
Kate Kinsley: Protecting Ava
Rayne Lewis: Justice for Mary
Heather Long: Securing Arizona
Margaret Madigan: Bang for the Buck
Ellie Masters: Sybil's Protector
Trish McCallan: Hero Under Fire
Kimberly McGath: The Predecessor
Rachel McNeely: The SEAL's Surprise Baby
KD Michaels: Saving Laura

Lynn Michaels: Rescuing Kyle

Olivia Michaels: Protecting Harper

Wren Michaels: The Fox & The Hound

Annie Miller: Securing Willow

Kat Mizera: Protecting Bobbi

Keira Montclair: Wolf and the Wild Scots

LeTeisha Newton: Protecting Butterfly

Angela Nicole: Protecting the Donna

MJ Nightingale: Protecting Beauty

Victoria Paige: Reclaiming Izabel

Anne L. Parks: Mason

Debra Parmley: Protecting Pippa

Danielle Pays: Defending Sarina

Lainey Reese: Protecting New York

KeKe Renée: Protecting Bria

TL Reeve and Michele Ryan: Extracting Mateo

Elena M. Reyes: Keeping Ava

Deanna L. Rowley: Saving Veronica

Angela Rush: Charlotte

Rose Smith: Saving Satin

Lynne St. James: SEAL's Spitfire

Dee Stewart: Conner

Harley Stone: Rescuing Mercy

Sarah Stone: Shielding Grace

Jen Talty: Burning Desire

Reina Torres, Rescuing Hi'ilani

Savvi V: Loving Lex

Megan Vernon: Protecting Us

LJ Vickery: Circus Comes to Town

Rachel Young: Because of Marissa

R. C. Wynne: Shadows Renewed

Delta Team Three Series

Lori Ryan: Nori's Delta

Becca Jameson: Destiny's Delta

Lynne St James, Gwen's Delta

Elle James: Ivy's Delta

Riley Edwards: Hope's Delta

Police and Fire: Operation Alpha World

Freya Barker: Burning for Autumn

B.P. Beth: Scott

Jane Blythe: Salvaging Marigold

Julia Bright, Justice for Amber

Anna Brooks, Guarding Georgia

KaLyn Cooper: Justice for Gwen

Aspen Drake: Sheltering Emma

Emily Gray: Shelter for Allegra

Alexa Gregory: Backdraft

Deanndra Hall: Shelter for Sharla

EM Hayes: Gambling for Ashleigh

India Kells: Shadow Killer

CM Steele: Guarding Hope
Reina Torres: Justice for Sloane
Aubree Valentine, Justice for Danielle
Maddie Wade: Finding English
Laine Vess: Justice for Lauren

Tarpley VFD Series
Silver James, Fighting for Elena
Deanndra Hall, Fighting for Carly
Haven Rose, Fighting for Calliope
MJ Nightingale, Fighting for Jemma
TL Reeve, Fighting for Brittney
Nicole Flockton, Fighting for Nadia

SEAL Team Hawaii Series

Finding Elodie

Finding Lexie

Finding Kenna

Finding Monica (May 2022)

Finding Carly (Oct 2022)

Finding Ashlyn (TBA)

Finding Jodelle (TBA)

Eagle Point Search & Rescue

Searching for Lilly (Mar 2022)

Searching for Elsie (Jun 2022)

Searching for Bristol (Nov 2022)

Searching for Caryn (TBA)

Searching for Finley (TBA)

Searching for Heather (TBA)

Searching for Khloe (TBA)

The Refuge Series

Deserving Alaska (Aug 2022)

Deserving Henley (Jan 2023)

Deserving Reese (TBA)

Deserving Cora (TBA)

Deserving Lara (TBA)

Deserving Maisy (TBA)

Deserving Ryleigh (TBA)

Delta Team Two Series

Shielding Gillian

Shielding Kinley

Shielding Aspen

Shielding Jayme (novella)

Shielding Riley

Shielding Devyn

Shielding Ember

Shielding Sierra

SEAL of Protection: Legacy Series

Securing Caite (FREE!)

Securing Brenae (novella)

Securing Sidney

Securing Piper

Securing Zoey

Securing Avery

Securing Kalee

Securing Jane

Delta Force Heroes Series

Rescuing Rayne (FREE!)
Rescuing Aimee (novella)
Rescuing Emily
Rescuing Harley
Marrying Emily (novella)
Rescuing Kassie
Rescuing Bryn
Rescuing Casey
Rescuing Sadie (novella)
Rescuing Wendy
Rescuing Mary
Rescuing Macie (novella)
Rescuing Annie

Badge of Honor: Texas Heroes Series

Justice for Mackenzie (FREE!)
Justice for Mickie
Justice for Corrie
Justice for Laine (novella)
Shelter for Elizabeth
Justice for Boone
Shelter for Adeline
Shelter for Sophie
Justice for Erin
Justice for Milena

Shelter for Blythe

Justice for Hope

Shelter for Quinn

Shelter for Koren

Shelter for Penelope

SEAL of Protection Series

Protecting Caroline (FREE!)

Protecting Alabama

Protecting Fiona

Marrying Caroline (novella)

Protecting Summer

Protecting Cheyenne

Protecting Jessyka

Protecting Julie (novella)

Protecting Melody

Protecting the Future

Protecting Kiera (novella)

Protecting Alabama's Kids (novella)

Protecting Dakota

New York Times, USA Today and *Wall Street Journal*
Bestselling Author Susan Stoker has a heart as big as
the state of Tennessee where she lives, but this all
American girl has also spent the last fourteen years
living in Missouri, California, Colorado, Indiana,

and Texas. She's married to a retired Army man who now gets to follow *her* around the country.

www.stokeraces.com
www.AcesPress.com
susan@stokeraces.com

Made in United States
Cleveland, OH
04 October 2025